SARAH ARNETTE

Dragon's Pet

Unseen Treaties

To the Dreamers hoping for Dreams to really come true.

Contents

Acknowledgement

I'd like to thank Rob for his constant patience. He has heard more about this story over the years than anyone should ever have to endure, and he has never complained.

WriterDojo and Authors Unite have done more to get this book written than they can ever image. Thank you for encouraging me and putting up with my teasers.

Nathan and Book Club, you guys are the best. Love you all.

1

Chapter 1

Germany is boring. Life is boring. My life is boring. At least that is what Ansel thought as he cut wood for what seemed like the millionth time that fall. How much wood could one family need? Here I am, chopping wood, when I should be getting ready to go out with Beno to cruise for women. No... I have to be chopping wood. Life just is not fair sometimes.

Just as Ansel grabs the last bundle of wood that he is planning on splitting that day when Beno comes swinging down the drive in his car, looking cheerful and relaxed as always. He has responsibilities, just like everyone else, he just somehow manages to look like he doesn't. His brown eyes are always cheerful and bright, his brown hair is always styled and soft. It does not hurt that Beno is tall and built with that solid strength of a natural athlete.

Ansel is not bad to look at either, at least according to the women that they meet. He is not quite as tall as Beno, but his eyes are darker, as is his hair. Most women, and quite a few men, are impressed with his shoulders, broad from constant work on the farm. His waist is well tucked and he even has a butt, from all of his time squatting down to work on fences. The farm life might not be easy, but it does build a nice body.

Ansel's shy personality is usually the winning feature though, and that might be why he gets along so well with Beno and his outgoing nature. Ansel gives Beno someone to bounce his light off, while Beno gives Ansel the confidence to put himself out there. Beno is head strong and often likes to follow the plans that he makes, Ansel is very easy going, often willing to just go with the flow. They have been best friends since they were little.

"Give me a minute to clean up, then we can head out," Ansel calls out to Beno even before Beno leaps out of his Volkswagen. It is a silver coup. Ansel would be hard pressed to remember exactly what model. Beno seems to go through cars like women go through shoes, as the saying goes. Not that he had ever noticed his mother or sister going through a lot of shoes. *Maybe they are the exception?*

Ansel would have preferred a shower, but he does not have time for all that, so a quick wash of his face and hands, a new shirt, and they are out. Besides, women like that rugged, dirty look sometimes, or at least that is what Ansel tells himself as he looks at Beno's immaculate outfit. Beno likes to dress to impress, even if the only one he is impressing is himself.

Tegernsee is not a big city. It is actually incredibly small in comparison to the cities that surround it. An hour from Munich, it is a tourist trap of a town with large luxury hotels along its small lake. Surrounded by woods, it looks like the perfect escape, and for two twenty year old men, it is the perfect place to sow some wild oats. There are always some young women looking for attention and affection staying at the expensive resorts that are the city's primary source of income, usually the wealthy children of Munich business men. It is perfect for a fun night and no regrets in the morning.

This night is no exception. Ansel and Beno have the time of their lives once again, partying and playing with the wealthy and bored. The small hours of the morning come and go without notice as they dance, drink, and love without discretion. It is only as the sun rises on that fall morning that they finally find their way back to Ansel's farm to recover.

After a quick nap at the kitchen table and some coffee, it is time to get ready to do the farm chores, again. They had come home to a list made by Corrinne, Ansel's mother, of what chores needed to be done first that day. She always makes sure to make a list and have it ready the night before so Ansel and Hannah, his older sister, cannot claim ignorance of their chores.

Looking over what needs to be done, Ansel almost looks defeated. The list goes on and on, sometimes even including the instructions for the task, as if Ansel has not been doing those same chores for the better part of a decade. Being the only boy in the small family, he does most of the heavy work. His sister might be milking and feeding the cows, but he is chopping wood, tilling fields, and fixing fences. This has been and will likely always be the way their family is run.

They have to get moving pretty soon. His sister might not disturb him and Beno at the table, but Corrinne is something different altogether. She would not feel bad for their hangovers. She has no patience with foolishness, as she sees it. Anything that could be construed as fun is foolishness to her. If Corrinne catches them loafing at the table they would suddenly be finding new chores, even Beno. Beno has argued that he does not live at the farm and therefore should be exempt from chores, but Corrinne simply answers that he is there so often, he might as well live there.

Looking over the list, Beno makes a decision that getting more wood would be first on the list and he would help. "Wood. Wood will be easy to get, and then we can work on the fence. After that, I have to head home and get some work done there. I'll be back after dinner." Beno sets down the list and smiles at his best friend. A load shared is a load eased.

Ansel knows that this will be bad, but hey, at least it will be fun. Beno has a tendency to get distracted, not that Ansel minds. Piling into Ansel's car, they head into town in search for more wood to satisfy Ansel's mother's fears that they won't have enough. It's not like they don't have the Dragon Forest right behind their property or anything.

Chapter 2

Tegernsee is small. Tegernsee is focused on being a tourist town. Tegernsee does not have too many large stores or specialty stores for camping supplies. Tegernsee does not have any bundled wood available. It has all been bought up by the different luxury hotels that dominate the town, for their in-room fireplaces. Nothing but the best for their guests. Unfortunately, that means that Ansel and Beno are not coming home with the necessary wood. *Maybe mom won't notice? It's not like a huge pile of wood wasn't dropped off just last week.* Ansel thinks to himself as he rides in the passenger seat of Beno's car.

Beno and Ansel head home after picking up groceries, the third thing on the list of chores for the day, deciding that while the fence is important, there was no sense in going out twice. The fence could be item three, but Ansel was going to have to work on it alone. Beno has to get going.

Dropping off Ansel with his groceries, Beno does not even put the car in park while Ansel unloads it. He knows that if he gets out of the car, Hannah or Corrinne will give him work to do. Instead, Beno heads off to his own home in the city to clean up and get his own work done. Ansel, meanwhile, heads off to fix fences, move things, and get the farm ready for winter. It will take weeks, but he will get it. He always does. *If I'm lucky, I'll get a nap before Beno comes back for our nightly rides,* Ansel thinks, as he crosses off items four and five. At this rate, he might even be able to find himself some time to read. He is making very good progress on his list.

Unfortunately for Ansel, Corrinne notices that the wood pile did not increase. In an uncommon bout of discipline, she forbids Ansel from going out with Beno until more wood is cut and added to the pile. "You never know how much wood winter will need. I do not want you trying to gather and split wood in the middle of winter. It is too dangerous. It is better to get the wood now, while it is still fall. How can I trust you to make good decisions while you are out, if you cannot be responsible for something as small as a wood pile?"

"You are comparing going out with Beno for an evening with being able to find wood? Mom, be reasonable. I am going to get you the wood, but it will be tomorrow. I have to go to Munich for it. Do you want me to make the hour drive now, at night, to spend an hour finding wood in the huge city, and then drive an hour back? Or would you rather I just wait until tomorrow morning to go into the city?" Beno counters her argument.

"Do not attempt that round of logic with me. If it were just the drive to Munich and back you would not hesitate. Instead, you want to run around with Beno, getting into who knows what trouble. I was young once, too. I know what goes on between young adults. No, you choose to put this off, and now you will be choosing to stay home for the night," Corrinne insists and her word is law.

"How about I just go into the woods, and gather some deadfall? It would not take me very long at all to do so. It'd be quick, easy, and safe. I will keep the house in sight, so there would be no chance of getting lost," Ansel tries an old argument. For some reason, he has never been allowed in the woods. He is pretty sure that his Mom would rather relent than risk him going into the forest, for some reason.

"No, and you knew that the answer was going to be no before you asked. Manipulation does not become you. You know that the forest is haunted and dangerous. You are never to enter it. You are never to interact with anything that comes out of it. You know this. You will not go out tonight, and that is final," Corrine slashes her hands through the air in an X pattern as she speaks. To say that Corrine is emphatic is to understate the situation.

Neither Ansel, nor his sister Hannah, or Beno for that matter, actually believe this line of superstition from their mother. They humor her. She has never been the same since their dad walked off and she blames the forest for that. She blames the witches and the evil eye for bad harvests, and God Forbid if the truck breaks. She does not know which evil spiritual entity is responsible for that, so she blames all of them at different times.

Some of it seems true, at least. There have been instances that they could not explain logically, and they each had their own beliefs as to which of the superstitions are accurate versus chance. They believe some of her superstitions, a bird in the house means someone will die, to not wish someone an early happy birthday. Those are true, but an evil, soul-devouring spirit in the woods? Not so much.

Ansel is washing up as Beno swings into the driveway. Without knocking, Beno enters the kitchen, having all but grown up in that house with his best friend. It only takes one glance to tell that something is wrong, Ansel is not ready to go out that has become their habit. He is in his house clothes, a worn pair of jeans and a flannel shirt. He looks like an American hillbilly. "What's wrong? Not going out tonight?"

"Nope. Mom says not until we have more wood for the woodpile. I tried to explain that there is no more wood in town. I told her that I'd swing down to a bigger town tomorrow and buy all the wood I could find, but she isn't listening," Ansel complains as he leans against the sink. He is holding a towel in his hands. He had just gotten finished washing the dishes, a chore he traded Hannah for a favor at a later date.

Hannah sat in the living room, reading her latest fantasy book, Dragon's Ring by Dave Freer. She is greatly enjoying it and is not at all inclined to visit with Beno. Ansel can hear his mom getting ready for bed, even though the sun is barely down. The house is settling down, and soon he will as well. His body could use the rest. Dancing and drinking all night, then working all day can take a toll on anyone, Ansel included.

Quietly, so quietly, Beno whispers so Hannah does not hear him, "Let's gather some from the woods, we'll work together and chop it up and then head out. We'll tell your mom that I brought some over from town. No harm

6

done, and we both get to go out." Beno may be devious sometimes, but not even he is willing to risk Ansel's mom's wrath or cross her superstitions with her knowing about it. But what she doesn't know can't hurt her, right?

Ansel thinks about this, turning to check and make sure that Hannah is lost in her book, and not listening to them. *I know, KNOW, I should say no. I KNOW this will bite us in the ass, hard. I know that one night of actual sleep would be good and that my liver would thank me for a night without drinking, but I KNOW that going out is fun. Besides, what harm could it really be? The sun might be down, but the sky is still light and will be for a while longer. They won't be gone long, it won't take long to get one downed tree and cut it up. Oh, the evils that are Beno's temptations.* The angel on his right shoulder quickly loses to the devil on his left.

"Fine, but we move quickly and we don't go far into the woods. I might not believe Mom's claim of evil spirits, but I do believe that people get lost all the time in dark woods and I have no intention of being one of those people." Ansel whispers his agreement, pushing himself away from the sink, turning and throwing the towel into it. *I will have to clean up again after we get back, but it shouldn't take long. I have a clean shirt and jeans sitting on my bed, so we'll lose some time, but not much. It's not like the parties start until after midnight anyway. Anything before that is just the warm-up.*

The two men grab a couple beers from the counter and step outside, not bothering to be quiet about that. After all, if they are quiet about something like that, everyone will know they are up to something. They almost casually head towards the forest line with Ansel grabbing an ax and tossing Beno the rope as they go. Do not act suspicious, no one will get suspicious, and they will get away with this little scheme.

3

Chapter 3

I t did not take long for Ansel and Beno to make it to the woods. The field might be large, but they are strong men who are used to moving with purpose. Soon they are standing at the edge of the tree line. It is almost dark, the sun not quite set yet, but not too dark. It looks so much darker just past the tree line.

They stand there for a second in indecision. *After all, would it really be so bad to miss one night, to stay in just this once and do this in the morning or even drive to Munich to get wood? Our livers and heads might thank us if we went home.* Ansel thinks to himself, *No, I do not want to seem to be the coward, even just in front of Beno.* So with a single glance at each other, they enter the woods.

It is dark. Not pitch, but dark. They can see their hands in front of their faces, but they cannot see more than ten feet in front of themselves. Ansel is prepared and pulls out his flashlight, sweeping it around as they start looking for a downed tree, or at least one that would be easy to down. Cutting a tree down in the day can be dangerous, at night it could be *deadly*. Ansel is really hoping to find some deadfall and save himself the trouble.

It does not take long to find a tree, maybe thirty feet into the forest itself. The men can not see the house, or the barn, or the edge of the field for that matter, but that does not bother them that much. They can see their goal right before them. *How could we possibly get lost? We walked straight in, we'll just walk straight back, no problem. We know where we are and where we are going. We are not new tourists looking for an adventure, we are experienced men who are familiar with this area,* Ansel thinks to himself as he looks back in the direction that they came from. They had gone further into the forest than he was planning on going.

Half an hour later, the tree is tied up and ready to be moved. They cut it into manageable pieces, but there is still some work to be done in the morning. It would be done enough to prevent too much trouble with Ansel's mother when she finds out that they went out. *Mom always finds out when I go out.* Now just to get out of the woods. With a smile at Beno, Ansel turns around and heads back the way that he came. Or so he thinks.

After a few minutes, it is apparent that Ansel and Beno are going the wrong way. They should have easily come to the edge of the woods from where they found the tree, but they could not even see it from where they were. Yes, it is dark, but it does not seem like it should be that dark.

They walk a few more minutes the same way, and then decide to turn to their right, figuring that they will find their way. They could not have been that far off from where they thought they were, and right seems as good as left. After all, if they do not find the field shortly, they will just turn around and go the other way. It is a testament to how well the two men know each other in that they did not have to talk to make any of these decisions.

Half an hour later, they are still no closer to finding their way out. The wood that they are carrying is beginning to get heavy and a deep darkness has descended upon the men. They are actually beginning to get a little nervous about getting out of the woods before morning. The noises of the forest begin to make them jumpy, adding to their disorientation. Every crack and rustle of the branches around them seems to echo in their ears.

They unconsciously move ever so much closer together, walking almost side by side, taking comfort in each other. They have handled everything together, they will handle this together, too. It is almost like the forest is moving. The trees shifting to keep them from ever finding home. The tree that they haul with them seems to gain weight, and fear truly begins to set in. Ansel keeps wiping cold sweat from his face, terror making him clammy.

Just as they are about to give up, they caught movement out of the corner of their eyes. Both of them spin their heads, twisting their bodies so that they are facing the sudden motion. Their eyes are wide and their breath is ragged with fear. Ansel feels the need to take Beno's hand in comfort, just like he did when they visited the haunted house when they were children. He resists the urge though, afraid that Beno would reject him.

"What was that?" Ansel spins around, trying to see what he thought he saw, the dark making him jumpy. The bundle of wood on his back throws him slightly off balance and he staggers, trying to keep his balance.

"Truthfully? I thought I saw a girl," Beno answers a little sheepishly. There is no way that there could have been a girl in those woods, not at this time of the night. But then, Ansel often accused Beno of seeing women where there were none.

"A girl? Or a woman? Was she a ghost?" Ansel teases. He is nervous and scared. Teasing Beno was more to relieve his anxiety than to get a reaction from Beno, which is good because Beno ignores his questions.

They walk on a little longer, a little slower, a little more cautious. Being anxious is not helping their mindset. They are soon jumping at every snapped twig, turning at every imagined ghost. Their breaths are ragged, and their hearts pounding. Their burdens are all but forgotten except as extra weight slowing them even further down and causing them to stumble. It is then that they see her.

4

Chapter 4

She is lovely, otherworldly in appearance. She is dressed in a simple white shift dress, older in style but not a traditional German dress that is sometimes common around town. The sleeves are loose along the shoulders, but tighter at the wrists and forearms. The waist is cinched just under her breasts, and the skirt flows in waves down her body. The tops of her bosom are bare, exposed to the cool night air. Her skin glows like alabaster. Her silver hair all but shimmers in the darkness, and her blue eyes are so piercing that seeing them is akin to looking at stars. She looks like she is in her early twenties. Ansel and Beno stop and stare. They are seeing the ghost of the Dragon Forest, they are sure of it.

The woman, ghost, apparition of some sort, looks as though she is gliding through the woods. She takes her time walking through the woods, trailing her arms behind her, turning, spinning and dancing. She looks like magic come to life. She is entrancing to gaze upon. To say that she looks like she just stepped out of a fairy tale is not an exaggeration.

"What are you doing out here? Are you lost?" the woman asks, a puzzled look crossing her face, when she notices the men. Ansel and Beno are too startled to say anything. They did not know that ghosts could talk and interact with the living. When no answer came, she addresses the men once more. "Cat got your tongue?" the woman teases, musically, and lightly. *For a ghost, she is quite friendly and quite beautiful*, thinks Ansel.

"Ahhh....," Never speechless Beno answers.

"Are you the ghost?" Ansel asks her, immediately feeling like an idiot. *If she is a ghost, she might not know that she is one, or she might get angry. Didn't my mother teach me not to interact with ghosts, spirits, or any other supernatural creature? I simply couldn't think of anything else to say, and to say nothing seemed just too rude,* Ansel berates himself. Good thing it is dark so he can hide his flushed cheeks. *I guess it is better than saying "you're beautiful" or some other type of nonsense that she has likely heard a thousand times,* Ansel has to admit, asking if she is a ghost is not the worst thing that he could have said.

Luckily for him, she just laughs, a light airy bell of a laugh. "A ghost? Really?" She reaches out and pinches him lightly. "Do I feel like a ghost?"

When did she get so close to us? Ansel thinks. He had not noticed her stepping closer to them. He could clearly remember her being at a distance, dancing in the moonlight, and now she is standing directly in front of him. Did she just appear there, or did she walk and him just not notice? "No, I guess not," Ansel's boyish grin appearing as she lightly flirts with him. Ansel never expected to be flirting with a woman in the Dragon Woods, but here he is, and she is definitely flirting. Ansel takes a step back, giving himself a little bit of room between him and the beautiful, but strange, woman. Beno is still in shock, looking back and forth from Ansel to the woman.

"Seriously though, what are you doing here? Are you lost?" The woman's voice suddenly turns serious as she drops her arm from Ansel. She sounds concerned, but not for her safety as she stands in the dark forest with two men. She sounds worried for them. That gives the men a bit of a pause.

"Actually, yes, we are lost," Beno finally finds his voice. "Ansel here," Beno gestures to his friend, "lives on the edge of the woods, and we needed to get some wood so stepping in to get a tree seemed like a good idea at the time. Alas, we must have gotten turned around because we can't seem to find our way out."

"By the way, I'm Ansel, and this is Beno," Ansel pipes up, realizing that they had not introduced themselves to this woman that they were now looking for assistance from. *Mom would be so pissed. First of my bad manners, and then about me giving our names to a possible supernatural creature. If she ever*

12

finds out about this, I am so dead, Ansel thinks to himself immediately after speaking up.

"Oh, well, I'm Schwarz and my house is just over there." She gestures back the way that she came from. "I can let you guys follow me to my house, have a sit down, then we can figure out where you guys need to go to get home. Come on, follow me."

The woman known as Schwarz almost bounces away from them, leading them what they are sure is is further into the woods. Her footsteps are sure and her bearing is confident, bare feet flashing. If it were not so impossible, Ansel and Beno could almost believe that Schwarz lead people through the woods, at night, in the dark, all the time. She obviously grew up in these forests, to be so sure of where she is going. She also must practically be able to see in the dark, not to trip on any roots or branches as she walks. She must be magic to keep her dress so pristine.

They did not know that there were any houses in the Dragon's Wood, but according to Schwarz, she lives in one. Being so young, they are sure that she likely lives with her family. They can only hope that whoever she lives with is amendable to them showing up in what feels like the middle of the night, even though it is likely not even twenty-two hundred hours. There is only one way to find out. Ansel and Beno glance at each other, unsure as to what to expect, but having no better options, follow this woman, named for the color black.

5

Chapter 5

S oon enough, without any misstep from their guide, Ansel and Beno come across the house that Schwarz promised. As one would expect in the middle of the woods, the house is rustic in appearance. The wood the house consists of has a rough look to it, while the details of the house promise a taste of refinement that one does not find in modern homes.

There are small engraved flowers and animals along the door and window frames. The door itself is completely engraved with what appears to be a lattice design with various people and animals hanging though the diamond sections. It is absolutely wondrous and unexpected from a cabin in the middle of the woods. It feels like it belongs in a castle. Ansel barely has a moment to glance at it before he is ushered inside.

Without a backward glance, Schwarz leads Ansel and Beno into the house. It is a study in comfort. The couches and chairs are overstuffed and have thick, warm-looking blankets draped over them. The fireplace is large and a small fire is roaring comfortably behind a grate. There is a kettle near the flames, keeping what Ansel presumed to be tea, from the smell of it, warm. The kitchen and living rooms are brightly lit with candles and open, making the small home appear large and luxurious. The whole place even smells inviting. It is almost as though Schwarz knew that she would have company and had made the place comfortable for them. *To live like this all of the time must feel wonderful, a permanent retreat from the world*, Ansel thinks.

"Tea?" Schwarz asks as she swings the kettle further from the fire, lifting it from its rack.

"Yes, thank you," Ansel answers, being immediately remembering his manners.

Beno is once again wearing his shocked expression, not expecting such warmth and comfort in the middle of the cold woods. His eyes keep flicking back and forth, taking in the rooms, Schwarz, and Ansel. He looks like he is having a hard time believing everything that has happened so far.

Really though, how could a comfortable home be more surprising than finding a friendly woman in the middle of the woods, in the dark? Maybe he is just scared or uncomfortable, Ansel thinks to himself as he sips the tea that Schwarz hands him. He normally drinks his tea with cream and sugar, but this one is perfect straight. He will have to remember to ask her what the blend is. Glancing back to Beno, he begins to worry about his friend's frame of mind. *After all, this was about as far away from our normal night activities as you can get. Well, besides being in a strange woman's home. That is not that out of the ordinary, but still, this is all new territory.*

As Schwarz drinks the tea that she poured for herself, Ansel takes the time to look around the small living room. There in the corner is a large tapestry hoop. It appears that Schwarz was working on it just before she found Ansel and Beno, or maybe it just looks that way to Ansel since Hannah never leaves her needle in her projects. She is always too worried about the potential for rust marks. The needle that Schwarz left in her project is threaded with a dark green floss, marking her next stitch in what appears to be a dragon leaping above the forest.

The rest of the room is taken up by large overstuffed chairs and a matching couch. There is no television or other modern touches at all. It is surprisingly comfortable and inviting, even without the modern touches. It takes Ansel a moment to realize that there are not even any electrical outlets or lights. The whole place is lit by candles and mirrors.

"Okay, so why don't you guys tell me where you live, and I'll help you find your way home tomorrow morning," Schwarz suggests as she finishes her tea. Taking the cup from Ansel once he is finished, she walks into the kitchen to make up some food for the men before they even have a chance to ask about it.

Ansel raises his voice to be sure Schwarz can hear him while she works in the kitchen. The sounds of her chopping vegetables and meat was actually quite soothing, reminding him of home. He had not even noticed that he is hungry while he tried to find his way home. Now he is starving, and the thought of a sandwich is enough to make his mouth water. He watches as she nodded along with his words, putting together cold turkey sandwiches and fresh vegetables. "It is right between the Reiderstein "Y" branches. My farm is the only farm out that way, between the main city and this forest."

"What do you mean, tomorrow morning?" Beno asks once she makes it back to the living room with two plates of food.

"Well, we certainly can't go back out tonight. It is far too dark and there are many things that are far too dangerous to go up against in the woods. No, morning would be much better," Schwarz's voice is cool, calm, and matter of fact. She certainly sounds as though she knows what she is talking about and brooks no argument from the men. *She has lived in these woods for way too long to be complacent about them*, at least that is the impression that Ansel gets.

Beno rolls his eyes dramatically at Schwarz's announcement, but Ansel takes it in stride, eating his sandwich with thanks. Yes, his mother is going to kill both him and Beno, but Schwarz is right, the woods could be dangerous at night. Once the men are eating, Schwarz begins working on her embroidery. Her stitches are graceful and steady, speaking of years of practice and work. A comfortable silence quickly settled on the room. Schwarz reaches the end of her thread the same time as Ansel finishes his sandwich.

As soon as Schwarz pulls the needle through the back of the piece, she starts looking for her scissors. She is at the end of her yarn and her needle needs to be re-threaded to continue, but first she has to get the old floss off the needle. She begins to mutter to herself how she just had them, "Where could they be?" Finally, after a few minutes, she asks Ansel, "Do you have a knife on you? I seem to have misplaced my scissors." Knives do not cut yarn as well as scissors, Ansel knows this from his sister's mutterings, but they will do in a pinch.

Ansel reaches over with his sharp pocket knife, thinking to slice the floss right between her fingers. She holds it out to him, her breath held and eyes expectant. Ansel feels that he is on the cusp of something, but how could such a mundane event such as cutting a piece of floss change anything? Little does he know.

6

Chapter 6

As soon as Ansel's knife cut through the floss, Schwarz hands jerk apart and she gives a tight gasp. Her eyes were so blue, but presently they begin taking on a green light. Her pale flesh, darkens, her hair drops out, a dull silver pool cast about her feet. She stands suddenly, dashing her work to the ground with her sudden movement. Through all this, a smile of pure victory stretches across her face.

Schwarz continues up, beginning to grow and shift. Her hands and feet elongate and develop claws, thick and long. Her teeth sharpen and grow as her mouth changes, becoming a muzzle. Her smooth skin becomes thick scales and wings sprout from her back. They are terrible wings of dark skin stretched between long finger-like protrusions. The transformation may have been silent, but the crashing of the cottage is deafening. Her scream of ecstasy and victory rides over that noise, silencing the forest beyond.

***

Beno sees her transformation and grabs Ansel by the back of his shirt. Together they dive under a table, hoping for all the protection that the heavy oak table might provide them. Although, they both know that if the dragon that Schwarz has become wants them dead, no table would save them. They hide there, crouching together until the silence of the forest overcomes them and they realize that the destruction is done. Corrinne told them not to talk to supernatural creatures, and told them not to go into the woods. They should have listened to her.

When Ansel and Beno finally come out from under the table, they find a dragon, many times bigger than an elephant, possibly bigger than the cottage was, standing in what was the living room. Debris from the house is littered everywhere. The stars are clearly seen overhead, and only the fireplace with its mantle remains standing. He, and he is definitely a he, looks quite pleased with himself, his mouth curling up into a smile, showing off the whitest teeth that either of the men had ever seen before. He is dark, black in the starlight that was now streaming into the clearing that had held the house.

"Why, thank you, Ansel. I have waited a long time for someone to free me from my cursed existence in this tiny forest, living in the paltry house," the dragon that is Schwarz has a voice that rumbles through the surrounding landscape without being painfully loud. "I would offer you a boon, but I don't have anything I can really give you. Instead, I think I'll adopt you and Beno and keep you as I had kept others in the past. Would you like that? Traveling the world, seeing new things, being my voice in the cities as we go about, reigning in chaos and excitement."

As Ansel stares up at Schwarz, unsure as to what to say, Beno feels the need to act. He grabs the nearest piece of wood and swings it at Schwarz with all of his not inconsiderable might. He screams as he moves, gasping afterwards as if he expended great amounts of energy in his one and only attack, shattering the weapon.

Schwarz barely acknowledges the blow. Instead, he calmly looks down at Beno and lets his smile falter. "You really shouldn't have done that, my dear Beno."

With wide eyes, Beno realizes he was about to die. That his one act to try to save himself was ill-conceived and poorly executed. He turns and runs. He almost immediately falls on the debris that litters what was once the floor. Struggling to get up, he can hear Ansel scream as Schwarz lungs forward to devour him in a single snap. He did not even have the opportunity to realize the moment that he died.

"Why? Why would you do that?" Ansel cries up to Schwarz. "He was my friend!" Ansel's eyes stream tears and his mouth contorts in the pain and shock of losing his best friend of most of his life. It was so sudden, there was nothing he could do, but it did not stop him from feeling that he should have done something. This night was all too much for him and he drops into a crouch, trying to make himself smaller, invisible to the horrors he has just witnessed.

"Because he was rude, and he attacked me after I offered him a gift, even though it was rightfully your gift. You were the one who freed me, after all. Beno was not worthy of the treasures I will offer you. All you have to do is join me in my travels," Schwarz's voice is calm, soothing, and almost comforting despite the fact that all of the horrors that sprung from him.

"What if I don't want to travel with you? What if I don't want to be your 'pet?'" Ansel sniffs at the end of the word pet, trying to convey his disdain for the idea.

"Well, I'm not going to make you come with me. You humans make very poor pets when you are unwilling. I would let you go, but I would remember that you spurned my gift and your farm would be the first to burn. It would be better for you and your family if you just travel with me, be my eyes, voice, and guide in this new world. For as long as you ride with me, I'll spare your farm."

Blackmail, even if he does not know it by that word, comes easy to Schwarz. He knows how to make humans fall into line. He has had a lot of practice in keeping humans. Ansel would not be his first pet, and most likely will not be his last pet. Humans are so frail in comparison to dragons. Their lives are so short, too.

He knows he has this one and that in time, Ansel would see the wisdom of traveling with him. Heck, Ansel might even grow to love Schwarz, he has seen it happen before. Just as Schwarz expects, Ansel looks up to him with his tear streaked face and nods. What else could he have done? His family is at stake.

7

Chapter 7

"Well, since that is settled, we should get going. You haven't slept yet, and last I remembered, humans need sleep. Not to mention that I have not slept yet, either. So, we will have to move to somewhere where you can get some sleep. In order to do that, you need a saddle so you don't fall while I'm flying," Schwarz says in a calm and matter of fact voice. He seems to Ansel to have completely forgotten about Beno.

Ansel follows Schwarz's directions on finding and then fitting the saddle onto Schwarz's back. The saddle itself is more like a traditional pet carrier than a horse saddle. It is made of a heavy wood that is fashioned with ornate traditional floral panels on the outside. The inside is richly padded, although the material has some pretty heavy wear on it. The cushions were likely quite comfortable at one time, but looks to be considerably less so now. The material itself was at one time a rich red and green satin, now worn thin and faded from time and use.

Once the saddle is on, the straps that are to keep Ansel in place are obvious. Luckily for him, or unluckily, the leather straps that make up the carrier's harness are in excellent condition. Apparently in his human guise, Schwarz had taken good care of the leather. There would be no reasonable way to escape short of running and putting his family in danger. There will be no extra time to develop a plan. Even as Ansel thought about running away and hiding in the woods, he begins climbing aboard and into the carrier. With no preamble, not even making sure that Ansel is secure, Schwarz launches himself into the air.

Under the cover of night, the flight is uninterrupted and uneventful. It is only a short period of time before Schwarz brings them down to land, high in a mountain. Then it is a quick bound before he is in a spacious cave with all the opulence of the finest castles. "Hum, it is rather dusty, and apparently a couple animals decided to make their homes here, but, a little work and this place will sparkle again," Schwarz comments as he looks around his home. Ansel could not tell if Schwarz was talking to himself or to him, but then, he guesses it really did not matter. He makes no comment either way.

Ansel starts working on getting out of his carrier as soon as they walk into the castle, swinging around like a toy in a child's hands, as Schwarz looks around, almost oblivious to his rider. He has some magic on the castle, but it did not do enough to keep the place clean. Either that or maybe the magic wore off. It had been a long time since he was home. He should be glad that no other dragons or such ilk decided to make it their home. Not that a goblin in the halls would much surprise him. It was not until Ansel drops to the ground that Schwarz notices him again.

"Oh, are you okay?" Schwarz sounds actually concerned about Ansel as he picks himself off the floor. "Here, let me show you where your room is so you can get some sleep. Tomorrow I'll fly you down to the town to hire some help so we can get this place cleaned up. Plus I think you'll need to pick up food because any human food here is going to be centuries old."

With that, Schwarz turns down the great room and into a large hallway with multiple doors. The most ornate of those doors Schwarz opens with a handle in the middle of the door, swinging the door outwards, presenting a spacious, if stale smelling room. "Hum, if you like, you can sleep with me, but this will be your normal room. At least when we are in this part of the world," Schwarz comments when he smells the stale air and looks upon the accumulated dust.

"No, I think I'll make do here," Ansel answers. He steps inside, turning around to face the dragon and smiles. He keeps his body relaxed and his hands in front of him, like he is nervous. He tries to look grateful and tired. *I wish acting tired was harder than it is. I need to come up with a plan to get out of here and being dead on my feet is not helping,* Ansel thinks to himself, trying to act innocent as well as tired. The former part though, that is a hard act to sell. Grateful and innocent is not at all what he is feeling, quite angry and frustrated would be far more accurate.

He is not willing to spend the night with the psychotic dragon who just killed his best friend and has basically kidnapped him. No, he has a plan. He is going to try to get out of this, alive preferably. He is going to get to his home, get his family out of there, and find somewhere safe, away from this dragon. Matter of fact, away from ANY dragons. *America might be far enough. I have never heard of an American dragon. Besides, isn't America the land of opportunity? I'm sure we could find something to do there.*

Ansel steps in further, towards the bed this time, turns around and looks up at Schwarz appreciatively and smiles as Schwarz shuts the door, using the handle once again. As soon as the door latches, Ansel drops his gratuitous look like a bad habit and glares at the door, raising both hands in a middle finger salute. He swings back around and looks at the room and begins planning. There is no way that he can stay in that room. There is no way he can stay in this mountain. He was NOT staying with a dragon, and most definitely not with Schwarz.

An extensive search of the walls leads to finding two TINY windows. His head could not fit through them, but they at least can let in a breeze, so Ansel opens both of them. There are no secret panels. No hidden doors. No escape routes besides the large door that he came in through. There is not even a note in the closet from previous "pets." The place is escape proof.

There is a large trunk full of the girliest dresses that he has ever seen, shoved into the back of the closet. They have this vaguely French look and appear to be in very good condition for their apparent age. There is also a oversized poster bed with thick quilts. Ansel pulls the top one off, leaving a mostly clean sheet on the bed. Apparently bugs and vermin simply did not invade this room. There are some tapestries and a fireplace. The stocked wood looks like it might burn a little too well, so maybe not safe to use. *Besides, how clean is that flue, or would I be killing myself, firing that up?*

With nothing left to try, Ansel attempts the door. Well, he tries to attempt the door. There are no handles on his side of the door. The handle that Schwarz used is on the outside, and there is no way to open the door from the inside. There is barely even a gap between the door and the door jam to try to pry the door open with. Staring at the red inlay wooden door with its little flowers, the whole thing is just a little too surreal for him.

He slowly turns in place one more time, noting the rich red paneling, the fancy battle scene in the tapestries, and finally the canopy bed. The room does not even have a bathroom attached. A look under the bed finds a chamber pot. It was too much for him. With that, Ansel drops onto the bed and falls asleep. A new plan would have to be made in the morning. Maybe he would go to the village and simply not come back. Schwarz did say that he was going to take him into town to find contractors and whatnot.

8

Chapter 8

I t is late in the morning when Ansel wakes up. There is bright light crossing the room. There is something of a breeze, carrying with it the fresh smell of an autumn woods. Only once Ansel gets up and starts moving around does the door swing open, showing Schwarz on the opposite side of the door. "Great! You're awake." Schwarz moves away from the door and begins leading Ansel further into the cave.

The cave is one in name only. The walls are all beautifully carved. The doors are a thick wood with black iron hinges and rings for handles. They do not appear to latch, but rather fit snugly into their frames, staying in place due to their weight and fit. There are tapestries hanging on the walls, as well as some paintings. Heraldic banners hang beside the doors. It looks like a LARPing convention that actually acquired some money for their decorations and went crazy creating the most authentic fantasy castle they could. Everything is dusty and slightly dirty, but even through the dust and dirt, Ansel can see the expense that each item must have been.

"There is a kitchen, bathing room, and exercise court. There is also my room and some rooms for visiting dragons and humans. You have free reign to explore any of those rooms. Now, if you want, we can go to the city. I'm sure you must be hungry and I need some people to clean this place." Schwarz leads Ansel to the treasury. Using what appeared to be magic, small orbs began to emit a strong, but not glaring light.

"How much is food?" Schwarz is standing in front of a pile of gold coins and nuggets. Ansel had never seen so much gold in his lifetime and never hoped to see that much gold. There is not only the pile that Schwarz is standing in front of, but many other piles throughout the whole room. A single pile would more than pay for the family farm for generations. Ansel is dumbfounded.

"Ansel, how much does food cost?" Schwarz turns to look Ansel, watching him. He is used to this expression in his pets. Most of them never had so much gold in their city, let alone in their presence. Either that, or maybe this one is an idiot and did not know how much food costs. Both options are equally as likely, especially since he did find this one in the middle of a wood, at night. Brains might not be his strong suit.

"Um, they don't use these coins anymore. I'll have to get them exchanged for Euros. I'm not sure how much I will need," Ansel answers in a far away voice. Gold Stunned might be a good term for how he feels, standing in that room.

Schwarz frowns slightly, and grabs a medium sized leather bag and adds a substantial amount of gold to it. "Well, I had better give you more than not enough gold. I rather you be able to purchase your food and hire a good sized crew to clean all at once rather have to make multiple trips. Here, see if this is too heavy for you."

Ansel hefts the leather bag, strapping it to his back. He wobbles a bit, but was able to stand straight under the weight, barely. "Got it, I hope." He is afraid that if he takes it off his back, he might not be able to get it back on, so he follows Schwarz out with the bag still strapped to him. Unfortunately for his plan, he still needs to take the bag off so he could put the saddle back on Schwarz so they could fly down to the city.

Before they leave though, Schwarz goes back over the rules of the trip. "You need to purchase a cleaning crew, and food for yourself. You can also buy yourself some clothing and trinkets. If there isn't enough gold for that, we can see about going back down tomorrow, but I don't want you to expect daily trips to the town. The cleaning and food are most important today though.

"Now, if you are thinking that now would be a perfect time to run off, know that I will find you, and eat you. I will eat you, your family, your friends, and your village. Simple as that. Remember, you told me where you live. You will learn to love living with me, I can do a lot for you and your family if you are good.

"If you attempt to hire an army to destroy me, know that unless they possess magic, they can't harm me. Human magic users were rare a couple hundred years ago. I'm thinking they are even more rare now. Just be good, get what is needed, and enjoy this new life."

Ansel knows that Schwarz is not kidding or exaggerating. He would eat everyone that Ansel knows and that any plan Ansel might have, Schwarz has accounted for. *Besides, who would believe me if I said I was being held captive by a dragon.* He has no choice, just do as he is instructed and bide his time.

"If trips into Munich are going to become commonplace, might I simply buy myself a car? It would not need to be an expensive vehicle, just one to make it so I can get to and from town without bothering you?" Town, Munich, not quite the same thing, but whatever Schwarz wants to call it. A car would help him a lot. It would give him a sense of independence that he is sorely missing right now. He might even be able to negotiate returning home to see his family some time. A car would be much easier on his family than a dragon.

"Explain cars? Are they like horses?" Schwarz had spent 200 years in a forest. He is not up on all the new technologies, not that he had any wish to remain ignorant of them. Technology had always fascinated him. The electric magnet that Hans Christian Oersted created was absolutely amazing. It was like a piece of magic for the common folk to use. Schwarz could hardly wait to play with all the new technologies that the humans have created since his captivity.

"Ah, cars are like horses in that they make travel easier. But they are more like carriages in that they can carry a lot more than just one person and they are enclosed. They run on petrol, rather than food. They are made of metal and plastic rather than flesh and blood." *How to describe everyday items to someone who has never seen them before. Cars were cars, unless you've never seen a car.* Ansel is thinking that there might be a way to escape using Schwarz's lack of technology, maybe.

"This is something you will need?" Schwarz is a little skeptical. But, he did have a previous pet who needed a horse and time to explore on her own every now and again. Ansel might be the same type of person.

"I think it will be essential not only for everyday tasks, but for my overall happiness. There is a lot of joy to be had by being able to go out and get a cup of coffee when I feel like it," Behave like a pet, logic and emotion said nicely, and maybe he will get what he wants... escape.

"Okay, see what you need to get a car. A nice car that you will not need to replace right away. I do not want to have to buy a new car every time I turn around. We'll have to get the path to the Palace graded and cleaned up. Carriages could barely make the journey last time I was here, I doubt the path has gotten better with time. There was a riding path, it might work for your car. We'll be flying right over it. You can look out the saddle and take a look at it. Also make up a list this week of what needs updated. This place has to be made comfortable for both of us, and for the visitors that we will eventually be hosting."

Schwarz can let him have a car. It might make dealing with Ansel a little easier. The only problem with adopting adult humans as pets is that they often are already pretty well set in their ways. He would have to compromise with this one for a little while until he learned that Schwarz could be good to live with.

Chapter 9

The city that Schwarz lands on the outskirts of is Munich, a city that Ansel is rather familiar with. It happened to be where Beno and he would frequent when there was nothing going on in their hometown. Being only an hour away from Tegernsee, Munich was the easy second choice.

Ansel laments that those easy days and nights of hanging out in Munich with Beno are gone for good now. He fights not to tear up, looking down at the magnificent city, picking out their favorite haunts. Ansel does not want to make Schwarz suspicious that he might run any earlier than necessary.

"How did no one see us land?" Ansel fully expected to see a crowd of people flocking to their location. After all, while Munich has seen just about everything, her people have not actually seen a live dragon before, as far as Ansel knew. Although, thinking about it, it is Munich, there is a chance that the people there have seen a dragon before and would be unfazed by one appearing now.

"Oh, that's a simple piece of magic. It makes it so that people fail to notice what they are not expecting to see. Most magick-baring types of creatures have some type of magic like that. It's an active magic though. I have to think about it to use it," Schwarz answers off hand.

He almost did not use the magic, but dragons were rare 200 years ago, and he did not feel that the population has grown that much since then. No, he does not need a crowd of people flocking to him when he is not ready to host them yet. Besides, Ansel is too new to risk getting lost in a crowd. There is enough risk letting him go into Munich alone, but Schwarz could not see a way around that one.

It is convenient for Ansel, not being surrounded by people. Plus he knows where everything is in Munich. It would no time at all for him to find a bank to trade in the gold on his back for Euros that he could actually use, although the hike into Munich was a long one. He ends up flagging down a taxi and paying for the trip with the few Euros he had on hand when he had gone out to gather wood. Riding to the bank is much easier than trying to walk all the way there with 24 kilograms of gold in a backpack.

***

The look on the bank teller's face is priceless as Ansel carefully set down the bag full of gold. The look of incredulity quickly turned to a look of irritation though as the bag shatters the glass-topped counter and falls into the cabinet below it with the racket of broken glass and spilled coins. The bank, normally quiet, is suddenly, and jarringly, echoing with the sounds of breaking glass and coins bouncing along the marble floors. People cringe at the noise and many cast angry glares in Ansel's direction, as though he intentionally hurt their ears.

Picking up the coins is time consuming and calling in a specialist who could tell the purity of the gold is even more time consuming. Through it all, the bank teller remains calm and professional. She never once shot a single evil look in Ansel's direction, at least not one that he ever sees, besides that first one when he broke her counter. Even though he would have understood it if she did, he certainly deserved a few evil glares for the amount of work he put on their schedule, without so much as a by your leave. There is nothing like an absolute disaster to come rolling in to ruin a perfectly good day, and Ansel is absolutely certain that he is that disaster. The entire time, Ansel is just hoping that Schwarz will be patient.

Despite the trouble, it is not very long before Ansel walked out of the bank with 437,500 Euros and two shiny new bank accounts, each with a quarter million Euros in them. Hopefully, more than enough for a cleaning crew, food, and maybe some nice clothes. Ansel could not help but remember the beautiful dresses. If Schwarz's previous captives were well dressed, why shouldn't he be well dressed too.

There are a couple problems with hiring a cleaning crew, especially since he does not really have an address to give them. Then there is the problem of convincing them that they really would be cleaning a palace just outside of the city. No one had seen this palace, and one would think it would be noticeable. Instead he promises to meet them on the road closest to where they needed to go and then walk them in. Cash up front helps to convince them that he is serious.

With a cleaning crew quickly found and hired, food purchased, all of it shelf stable until he is able to determine what kind of refrigeration he has, with delivery scheduled for tomorrow it is time to have some fun. He is going to go shopping for himself, and if possible, his family. He plans on sending things home using the post office. He could not get permission to leave them, but he is hoping to get their forgiveness.

First, before he goes shopping, Ansel calls his family and gives them an excuse for where he is. He sorta found a new job, so that's what he told them, that he was now a purchaser for a wealthy individual. He also set up a checking account that they could draw from so that they would be more financially secure. With the house being just his sister and mother, money would quickly become tight. They would need to hire someone to help with the farm. Corrinne was never one to talk on the phone, so he gave Hannah all of the banking information over the phone.

After he gets that taken care of, it is time for a new wardrobe. The women that previously shared his room had trunks full of clothing. Ansel is not particularly fussy about his clothes, but having a few extra pairs of jeans, some nice shirts, and even a couple high end suits sounds to him like a well deserved luxury. He also picks up some higher end hygiene items and just about anything else he might need to live in the castle under the mountain. If he is going to be a pet, he is going to be a high maintenance pet.

The last part of the trip is buying a car. He was going to wait on it at first, but he has money to burn and he knows he needs a car sooner rather than later. Ansel already knows what type of car he wants, so shopping for one is going to be easy. He wants an Audi A3. It is a reliable sedan with decent fuel mileage. It is considered a luxury vehicle, but it is not so fancy as to make him uncomfortable with it. He was certainly not ready for anything like a Porsche, despite how pretty those are. No, the Audi is just what he needed. He picks a blue one, and plans on picking it up the following day. He would use that to guide in the cleaners and the delivery people.

At the end of his shopping trip, Ansel makes his way back to where he left Schwartz. The large dragon is basking in the sun, being the most obvious thing possible in the middle of a field. If this was how all dragons were, there must not be too many of them, otherwise Ansel would have heard of them before now, and not just in fantasy novels. Securing himself back into his saddle, piling all of his goodies in the carrier with him, they return home with a successful day behind them, forgetting to tell Schwarz that he would need to return to town and lead people to the castle for deliveries and cleaning.

10

Chapter 10

It was not until the following day that Ansel realizes something that should have come immediately to him, he did not buy food for Schwarz. He does not even know what dragons eat or how much that they eat. He could only hope that Schwarz does not decide to eat him. He should have thought about this while he was in Munich, maybe stopped at a library or something. *There have to be books about feeding a dragon, somewhere, right?*

He does not realize this in a sudden moment of clarity, he realizes it when he wakes up and begins heading out to meet the various people coming to do work for him. When Schwarz lets him out of his room, Ansel gets himself cleaned up, using cold water since heated plumbing has not been installed yet. When he wanders into the kitchen for breakfast, he remembers that he has no food for himself there. That is when he thinks about Schwarz, and the lack of food that Schwarz has, as well. He had also forgotten that he did not have a car yet. He would need Schwarz to get off the mountain.

"Where are you going?" Schwarz calls from a comfortable spot in the great room with a clear view of the surrounding countryside. He had not asked for change for the trip to Munich and did not ask what was purchased. He just assumes that everything is purchased as instructed and taken care of, and whatever little trinkets Ansel bought are worth it. More than one pet was turned from being afraid or hating him to loving him simply with some pretty toys.

Schwarz is a little concerned to watch Ansel attempt to stride right out the front door, fully dressed in new clothes, without so much as a word to him. He will have to stop him and find out what he is planning on doing. Raising his head off the padded bench he has been resting it on, he calls out to Ansel, stopping him right before he opens the front door, "We have to have things to do, today."

"What else do we have to do? I have to meet the cleaning crew and the grocery delivery people. It is not like there is an address here, is there?" It never occurred to ask if there was a postal number to this place, or a name or something that people might know about. It would have been helpful yesterday, but what is done, is done.

"We need to purchase cows and sheep for me to eat, or do you plan on me just hunting every day. That seems like more work than a cultured dragon such as myself to do. I am not making you hunt. Or did you do that yesterday, before returning to me and just forgot to tell me about it," answering Ansel's first question, Schwarz sounds almost irritated. That last question was not really a question. Schwarz knows full well that Ansel did not even think about it.

It dawns on Ansel that he had not eaten in a day, so Schwarz is most likely hungry. Schwarz continues before Ansel has a chance to answer him though, "And my last pet referred to this place as The Palace in the Mount, and everyone knew what that was. Are you telling me that no one down there in Munich remembered this place?" Schwarz's voice went from calm and quieter to almost angry and loud as he spoke. It was all Ansel could do not to crouch in fear.

"No, they did not know this place," Ansel answers carefully. A hungry, irritated dragon does not sound like something safe to be around. *I really hope that hangry is not a thing with dragons, but I'm betting it is.* He could not come up with a sufficiently dangerous comparison, but he is pretty sure that a Snickers would not help him. The image of Schwarz eating a Snickers bar and turning back into the beautiful woman that Ansel had first met flashes through his mind. It would be worth the attempt.

"Where do we get cows and sheep? Can we do this in the afternoon? I think I'm going to need more money than what you gave me yesterday." Cattle, sheep, and pigs are all expensive animals to buy, even in bulk. If they have to be killed and butchered, they will be even more expensive. Purchasing a farm is a possibility, that way they could breed the animals and hopefully make the initial investment pay for itself and limit the overall costs of running a farm of that type.

"It can wait until this afternoon, but not after that. I need you to purchase a farm. I like to eat a couple cows a day, and I've not eaten that way in quite some time. I think the first meal here will have to be a bit of a splurge for me. If the place has cows already butchered it would be ideal. A chef would also be a good piece of staff to get, so today or tomorrow you'll have to go back to Munich to hire a chef for yourself and me. I am not a fancy eater, but I definitely do enjoy well-cooked meat." Schwarz stalks back into the palace to get more gold, his mood foul.

Schwarz is not interested in entertaining a cleaning crew or whatever else Ansel has coming this morning. Instead, a nap might be a better idea for the morning. Besides, if no one remembers where this place is, they most likely do not remember that a dragon inhabited it. They would be afraid, and might not come back.

Wanting a nap and being hungry does not stop him from dropping Ansel off back at Munich though, trusting him when he said he would get himself back to his new home. He knows that Ansel has too much to lose to risk him running away. Besides, if the man becomes a bit more self-sufficient, then that gives Schwarz more time to just enjoy his company, rather than actually take care of him. Schwarz had forgotten how much work having a pet can be.

11

Chapter 11

When Ansel wakes Schwarz up shortly after noon, multiple people were working on the Palace. There are cleaning crews, plumbing crews, and kitchen crews. Ansel manages to get a bite to eat between directing the various crews, but he is a little worried that someone would walk in on Schwarz and quickly become a tasty snack. He is worried about himself becoming a snack. He knocks from the outside of Schwarz's bedroom door and peeks in when Schwarz answers him.

"Everything is going smoothly and everyone will be busy for hours. Now seems like a good time to head out, exchange gold for Euros, and find a farm for you. Do you want to fly down or would you like me to drive down to Munich and get it on my own?" Ansel calls from the door of Schwarz's room. He has no intention of going into the room or of startling Schwarz awake. If he can help it, he will never enter Schwarz's room. That feels too much like the fly entering the spider's living room for him. He does not want to become the snack of a hungry dragon as much as he does not want someone else to become a snack.

From the doorway, Ansel could see the great room that is Schwarz's bedroom. It is darker than his own room, a red so dark as to be almost brown. There is little in the way of furnishings. A large bed that is more akin to a pallet thickly lined with furs. There have to be hundreds of animals worth of furs in the makeup of Schwarz's bed. The walls feature tapestries, much akin to the ones in Ansel's room. The main difference in the tapestries is the content. Where the ones in Ansel's rooms are of battles, here they were of mythological creatures. The tapestries feature brilliant unicorns taking the fields, dragons in flight, and huge wolves that could be nothing short of the lycanthropes that the werewolf movies made so popular. These werewolves make those look like cuddly puppies though.

Off, along one wall, is a large shelving unit that is so cunningly built that it almost seems a part of the wall. It contains books large enough for a dragon to handle and various collections. There is a collection of human-sized shields that caught Ansel's eye in particular. He has to assume that they were from the various knights that tried to kill Schwarz and obviously failed. He will have to remember to ask about them sometime in the future.

"No, I will fly down with you. I will take in a little bit of hunting while I wait for you to finish your task. I don't much feel like sitting here in my room while people work throughout my home. It is making me irritated," Schwarz looks irritated. He looks hungry. Ansel is glad that he thought to ask rather than just leave. He is not sure if dragons could suffer from low blood sugar or if it made them more irritable like it does people, but he is not about to find out.

In short order, Schwarz is in his saddle and leading Ansel out the back way of the Palace so as not to frighten the workers. It is a bright, cloudless day on the mountain. There is a slight chill to the air, and Schwarz insists on Ansel dressing warmly for the trip, even though it was only a short flight, and so returns to Ansel's room.

Apparently, a former pet of his refused to dress for the flight, but rather dressed to impress and ended up freezing solid. Schwarz does not want to risk that again with his new pet. The only downside to this is that the only winter coats that are available were cut for women. Ansel did not think to buy a coat while in Munich and he certainly was not wearing one when he walked into the forest. Schwarz insists on Ansel wearing a coat, though.

Walking out of his room, Ansel is dressed in a fine woman's overcoat. He is not happy about it though. It is a brilliant emerald with a white fur trim. Despite its obvious age, it held together extremely well. The belt on it is wide

37

and the ends of the coat nearly brush the ground. The previous owner had to have been tall to wear this coat. The coat itself looks almost as though it could have been made especially for Ansel with the way it hugged his shoulders and tapered at his waist.

"I am not wearing this," Ansel declares, crossing his arms over his chest. The emerald and white trimmed accented the slight flush in his cheeks rather well, or at least Schwarz thought so.

"Why not? It evidently fits you. And if I remember correctly, it is a very warm coat. It should even have a matching scarf and matching gloves somewhere. There might even be a nice broach and hair comb that goes with it. Although your hair is a little short for the comb," Schwarz does not see the problem. He is hungry, tired, and he wants to get going. And yet, his new pet is holding everything up. It really is a very fetching coat on the man.

"Why not? It is a woman's coat!" Nothing could save the coat or make it manly. It is just short of flowers and hearts in its femininity.

"And? Everyone can tell you are a man. It is a coat. Put it on, be warm, and get in the saddle. If you insist, you can take it off before going into town."

Since when did Schwarz argue with his pets? He was much more used to them simply saying yes to whatever he wanted and going from there. This new breed of human is something else entirely. The matter settled though, Ansel agrees to wear the coat while flying, and that is it. It is not like he could really argue against the dragon. Not unless he wants to risk being Schwarz's first meal of the day.

12

Chapter 12

During their flight into Munich, Ansel notices that Schwarz is not really black as his name implied. Instead, the scales on his back are a deep green, as are his wings. They are not even a uniform green, but a rich cascade of dark greens, resembling deep forest leaves in high summer. Once they land, Ansel asks to see the underside of Schwarz, looking to see if that is also green, but no, it was the deepest of blues. There was truly no black on this dragon, known as Schwarz, the German word for Black. *How did I not notice this yesterday?* Ansel wonders to himself.

"Why are you named Black, if you are not black at all?" Ansel is completely perplexed. Once Ansel really looks at him, he would never mistake Schwarz's coloring for anything other than green and blue.

"Hum? My coloring has nothing to do with my name. My name, for now, is Schwarz, Black, due to my skills. I'm sure that my real name will come to me sometime, but I don't know any dragon that has gone by his hatchling name once leaving the nest. I haven't used my given name in a couple thousand years. We usually call each other, and ourselves, something that denotes a skill or feature we have. Sometimes even a personality trait. Names have power, even if it is not in a magical sense. We'll talk about it later. You have work to do," and with that, Schwarz dismisses Ansel to find a farm.

Ansel nods as he turns to walk into Munich, once again. He is not done thinking about what Schwarz said though. *I will definitely need to remember to ask Schwarz to explain magic to me. I feel like this is something that will become very important later on. The more I know about it, the better I will be able to avoid the hazards of it. I will also need to remember to ask about Dragons and magickal beings and their cultures. That will definitely come in handy. Too bad Hannah is not here, she probably already knows this stuff.*

It does not take long for Ansel to exchange gold for Euros and find a realtor. He explains that he is looking for a farm, cows, and sheep included, and wants to buy today. He explains that he has a large need for the cows and sheep, and was going to need the farm hands to stay on and manage the livestock. The realtor could not find a farm for sale at that time with everything Ansel needs, so they decide to visit a local large farm to see what they thought.

When they get to the farm, there is a bit of confusion. After all, why buy the farm when you can become the primary client? That would mean that the cost of the farm hands would be covered in the purchasing of the cattle, higher quality cattle could be purchased, and growth could continue without too much additional investment. Besides, what did Ansel know about running a large-scale farm? Sure, he ran his small family farm, but that is nothing like a commercial farm and the skills do not really translate. Ansel decides that the idea of being the primary client would be better, and purchases three cows and two sheep for the day and sets orders for more cows and sheep to be delivered every day to the Palace.

Then it was back to Munich where Ansel stops at the postal office. He could not keep calling the place he lives now, The Palace in the Mount. There has to be an actual postal code for it. Otherwise, people would not know where to deliver goods and services. A Post Office box is only good for the smaller items, he would need an address for the Palace. Surprisingly, the post office had a procedure and a postal code for various areas on the mountain. He is not the first one who opted to live away from the city. They quickly found the correct location and gave him a postal number and life is good, at least in that respect.

Telling Schwarz that he did not in fact buy a farm is a different story. Unsure if dragons could smell out lies, Ansel is completely honest with his reasoning as to why purchasing the cows and sheep was better than purchasing the farm. After all, if he purchased the farm, he would have to continually pay the workers, pay taxes on the land, pay for the food and supplies for the livestock, and all with no profit to be had from it.

This way, he could place large orders of cattle and have them freshly killed, prepped, and delivered every day to the Palace without any additional hassle. Besides, there is the whole management of a farm to deal with, and while his family owns a farm, he knows that he does not have the skills to run a cattle farm like Schwarz needs.

"We will try it your way, but the slightest failure on their part will mean severe repercussions on you and them. I do not like it when my instructions are not fulfilled," Schwarz sounds as grumpy as he is. He is hungry, and now his little human is being disobedient. He never had to worry about either thing with his last pets. This one is proving to be challenging. That is what he gets for adopting an adult stray, rather than raising one himself or contacting another Magickal for a youth from their stable, not that he had a lot of choice in the matter. He could not have let this one go, lost and and alone, back into the woods. Especially since he did release him from his curse.

Schwarz's mood lifts considerably when they get home to a clean front room and a note that the cleaning crews would be back to handle the bedrooms next. In addition, he is quite happy to see a live cow and to be informed that two butchered cows are in the cold cellars to be prepared for dinner. The live sheep is the honey on the spiced plums for Schwarz. Once he eats the three animals, he is in a much better mood and inclined to almost forget the disobedience of his Ansel.

13

Chapter 13

T he chef arrives later that day and begins cleaning the kitchen to within an inch of its life. He is excited to be a full time chef in such an amazing, if dated, kitchen. It had always been his secret dream to work in a castle and with truly antique appliances. There are multiple stoves and ovens. The freezers and refrigerators are old, relying on ice, but Ansel promises to update them as soon as possible. Ansel just needs to know what needs updating and how to best go about it.

The chef puts together a list of things that were necessary and another list of suggested items to take the kitchen from merely functional to exceptional and provides it to Ansel. It is an extensive list. Most of what is on there, Ansel cannot even identify. The number one item though, he knows, electricity.

The sinks that are in the original kitchen are adequate, or at least they were at the time. They are a limestone with a brass overlay. This worked when they were new, but they are not suitable for modern sanitations. Instead, Holdstock, the new chef, requests drawer style dishwashers. New refrigerators, warming drawers, roll-out shelves and racks, new ranges with new hoods, new ovens, and new stones for the built in fire ovens, all of this also went on the list. He also requested new lighting systems, needing to banish the dark and gloom from the kitchen. Ansel provides the list to Schwarz, who simply approves it and leaves it to Ansel to handle.

While the chef, a man by the name of Robert Holdstock, was unsure as to why he needed to cook a whole cow a day, he does not question it in the least. For as much as he is being paid to cook, he could forgive a large number of unique requests. If Ansel said that he wanted fish for breakfast and dinner at midnight, he would make it work. A whole cow, sheep, or pig a day was a lot of cooking, but not that much more than what he was used to doing, just for more people. This kitchen even came with a spit, so cooking a whole cow was not impossible or even difficult. The pulley system that was strung on the ceiling by a previous chef certainly helps, though.

He installs himself comfortably in the kitchen, promising to start cooking the next day, early for breakfast. He would cook breakfast and dinner every day but Sunday, making pre-prepared meals for that day. Lunch would be up to Ansel to provide for himself. To accommodate the large orders, he decided he would prep the animal so that half of it would be served for breakfast, and the other half for dinner. This made his life a little easier and gave himself a little more freedom of creation.

At Ansel's request, he even sets up a small kitchen that Ansel could easily use that would not be in Holdstock's way, that way Ansel could prepare himself food whenever he wanted. This kitchen includes a small range, oven, and refrigerator. Ansel does put in a luxury drink station, giving him access to perfect coffee, tea, and everything else at the flip of a switch. If he had to live in the Palace in the Mount, he was going to take every advantage of it that he could.

The process of cleaning and prepping goes on for some time before simple weekly maintenance cleaning is all that is needed to keep the place in good order. While many of the workers are curious as to just how Ansel could afford this level of luxury, even if there is no electricity, no one asks. It is never good to be rude to someone who is paying you a lot of money to do a job, even if it seems almost out of a fantasy novel. Their only complaint was the lack of electricity. Vacuums and electric steam cleaners were of absolutely no use. They had to do everything by hand.

Once cleaning is done, updates have to be done to the Palace in the Mount. This included electricity, indoor plumbing, and surveillance. The riding trail has to be paved, and one of the barns has to be updated for his new car.

The Internet has to be installed. The idea of getting internet while inside a mountain sent Ansel into giggles every time he thought about it, not that Schwarz understood the humor in it. Some parts of Munich proper did not have easy internet access, but Ansel will, while under a ton of stone.

Once the last bit of indoor plumbing is done, electricity ran, and the last speck of dust is gone, Ansel is able to fully appreciate the wonders that were his new home. The great room is stories high, with plenty of room for even Schwarz to stretch out in. The bedrooms have gold leaf accents and some of the richest wood that Ansel has ever seen. The library is extensive and well stocked with ancient works. He will have to get some modern books, but for now the old ones are at the center of his literary attention. The mirrors are all true silver, and the stone work is marble. The palace is nothing short of stunning.

It does not hurt that the chef underrated his skills immensely, preparing huge meals of beef and sheep daily as he is supposed to, but without losing the flavor and texture of small, intimate meals. Even Schwarz is impressed with the work of the various crews that have worked so diligently on his home, even if he did not get to watch any of them perform the work. It took months, but finally the Palace in the Mount feels like a home. Ansel even begins to feel as though it is his home.

It helped that he was able to talk with his mom and sister with his new cell phone without having to go all the way to Munich. He called the house almost every day, talking to Hannah at length about how to go about paying people to work on the farm and access the money that he provides for them through his bank account. Through a mutual understanding, they do not discuss what Ansel is doing to earn that money.

14

Chapter 14

One night, while Ansel and Schwarz are relaxing in the dining hall, eating their dinners, Ansel's a smaller version of Schwarz's, Ansel begins to ask questions. Questions that have been bothering him just a little bit and he could not figure out the answers to. Questions that none of the books in the libraries, public or private, seem to have the answers about. Questions about Schwarz himself. More specifically, Ansel wants to know more about the curse that he had some how managed to break.

"Um, if I may, why are you... Well, how.. Oh, there are so many questions I want to ask you, I'm not sure how to begin. After all, I know so little about you besides the fact that I found you, in the guise of a girl, in the Dragon Forest and that you had been under some type of a spell. How on earth did that happen?" Ansel finally decides that an origin story seemed like the best place to begin learning about his new owner/captiver/whatever you want to call him. *Isn't that how super hero movies introduce new characters, an origin story?*

"Hum... where to begin. Well, I was in that cabin, and the surrounding forest, because I was tricked by the elves. You see, I tended to be a bit of a trouble maker sometimes, and I may have eaten a prince because he was rude. In retribution, they went to the dwarves and had them fashion a chain of sorts. So, with a little bit of fairy magic, I think, they fashioned a spell that would mean that I would never get to finish my tapestry, because I couldn't cut the thread. The kicker was that the same thread bound me to that region.

"It had to be a complicated piece of magic, not something I readily understand since the Elves use such weird types of magic," Schwarz tells the story in a rather dry tone, with only minor resentment in certain spots, but all the story does is open up more questions for Ansel. So many more questions, but none of them are about Schwarz. These questions are about the world he now found himself in, a world that is much bigger and possibly more dangerous than he thought it was.

"Wait, there are elves, and dwarves, and fairies?" Shock colors Ansel's voice so it sounds almost childlike in its quality. His fork hovers just above his plate of food, halfway to his mouth. His eyes are huge, the cliche picture of disbelief. The fact that he is talking to a dragon and the irony of not believing in the other creatures never even touches him.

"Yes, there are elves, fairies, unicorns, dwarves, vampires, and the like. They all exist in different areas. Last I knew, and this was a couple hundred years ago, the elves went east, China I think. The unicorns went to Spain, Austria, and parts of Germany. The Dwarves spread themselves out in Italy. The Vampires went around Prague and some went to Rome of all places, and the Fairies hit this small island called Ireland. There are all kinds of non-human intelligences out there, all over the world. We can go meet some, if you like."

As if Schwarz is not already planning a trip to announce his re-emergence into the world. Especially to those troublesome elves. He will have to be careful though, there are some parts of the world where he is very much not welcome. He just got out of one curse, he most certain does not want to wind up the victim of yet another curse. There might not be such an obliging person around to help him this time. 200 years is quite long enough to be out of the world even when you can number your years in the the thousands.

"There are vampires? We can meet 'non-human intelligences'? How do people not know about these? Are there more dragons?"

"Well, most of the creatures have human pets that are bred from specific families for that purpose. This way when the pet is taken into the care of the dragon, unicorn, fairy, or whoever, there are no questions as to what happened to that person. Also, beings like elves, werecreatures, vampires, and dwarves can pass as humans. This helps to keep them hidden. Besides, you humans know about all this, you have stories and myths. You just didn't realize that they were all real," Schwarz sounds as though he was explaining to a child how the sky is blue. To him, all of this should have been common knowledge, but to Ansel, it is all new.

"Can we visit these beings?" Ansel is sold on his new life from this point on. A whole new life has quite literally been opened up for him. Fantasy is now real, fiction is now non-fiction. And he is going to experience it all. Hannah is going to be so jealous if she ever gets to find out about it.

"So, back to the curse. The thread that I cut with my knife. That was the chain that bound you to the region?"

"Yes. The dwarves are very good at creating chains that aren't really chains. That thread was one such chain. It did not physically attach to me, but it was tied to my magics, making it so I could not leave. I also could not cut it. I had to find someone else to do that. With the mythology surrounding the Dragon Woods, no one would come into the forest, which made it rather difficult to find someone to break the curse. It was certainly rather clever of them and showed a lot of interspecies cooperation," Schwarz answers with a tone that did not quite invite more questions without actually closing the topic.

"And then I came along," Ansel replies, looking from Schwarz to his food. He is also done with the topic. He does not like dwelling on that terrible night that Beno was eaten and his life was turned upside down.

"And then you came along," Schwarz agrees, turning back to his meal.

15

Chapter 15

After careful deliberation, Schwarz decides that the best first creatures for Ansel to meet, after dragons of course, are the Unicorns. This means a trip to Vienna, Austria. This is the home of the Spanish Riding School, and the home of the Lipizzan Horses. These light gray horses, so light in color as to be called white, are part unicorn, according to Schwarz, and have several unicorns in the various stables within the complexes that house the Lipizzans.

The flight from Munich to Vienna is not long, but the problem is the difficulty in finding the unicorns. Just because Schwarz knew where they were a couple hundred years ago, does not mean they stayed in that exact area or that the landscape did not change since then. It gets even harder when he realizes that he did not know how to contact them. It is simply by chance that one of the "pets" of the unicorns happens to see Schwarz fly above the stables, giving the unicorns the opportunity to find, signal to, and meet up with Schwarz and his new human.

Schwarz has just touched down outside of the Spanish Riding School, when one of the white horses from the riding school rode up to him. At least that is what it looks like to Ansel who notices the horse as a second thought to the stunningly beautiful woman astride the beast. As she touches the ground, sliding slowly from atop her mount, her light blond hair catches the sun and her blue eyes sparkle. As she walked towards the pair, her rust colored dress highlights long legs and a tiny waist. It is not until the horse talks that Ansel notices the horn on the horse's head.

Maestoso is the name of the unicorn standing before them. He was one of the founding stallions on what would come to be known as one of the most famous and powerful light horse breeds in the world. The Lipizzans are grace incarnate, intelligent, and long lived, all thanks to the unicorns. Maestoso is gray with his black skin covered in white hairs. His mane is long, his tail luxurious. His horn, now that Ansel was paying attention to it, was the color of Mother of Pearl and lightly spiraling from his forehead. His "pet," the graceful woman who so captivates his attention is Ősz.

"Greetings, Schwarz. I am Maestoso, and this is Ősz, my pet. It has been a long time since you have graced us with your presence. I see that you have been freed from your curse. Is this the one who has freed you?" Maestoso's voice is slightly accented and a little higher in pitch than Ansel would have expected, but it is still pleasant to listen to. The blue eye of the unicorn inspecting him like a bug is a little less pleasant.

Ansel is a little startled that Maestoro would know Schwarz, but then, why not, there is nothing to say that unicorns do not live forever, like it seems that dragons do. Ansel's initial surprise tapers down to pure acceptance, just going on for the ride. *Although, apparently, introductions as though they are newly met seemed to be the order of the day. It might have something to do with the time between meetings. Did unicorns change their names on a regular basis like dragons seemed to? So many questions, so little opportunity to address them in the moment.*

"Ah, Maestoso, it has been a long time. Yes, this is Ansel, and he is the one who freed me from the cursed Elven doings. Now, I keep him as a good luck charm and interesting pet. He really is quite fun and knowledgeable about this new world that I seem to have found myself in," Schwarz replies.

Ansel gets thinking to himself, *Schwarz obviously knew Maestoso from before his captivity in the German forest, although if they were friends, why didn't Maestoso send a pet to free him?*

As Maestoso and Schwarz catch up on the past couple hundred years, including two world wars and an attempt to conquer Europe by Napoleon,

Ansel decides to attempt to chat with Ősz. "Sooo... how long have you been Maestoso's pet?" *That seems to be the best way to start a conversation, right?*

Ősz looks up from playing with her nails and seems to have just noticed Ansel for the first time. Her face lits up with a smile, her eyes brighten, and a slightly breathy giggle escapes her lips. She captivates Ansel in a single moment. "Oh, I have been with Maestoso for my entire life. My mother is also his pet. All of the women in my family belong to Maestoso," she ends her answer with another slight giggle, as if this might be the silliest question she had ever heard. She sways back and forth, from left to right, keeping a smiling face to Ansel the entire time. She looks like a vision.

"Oh, well, I guess that makes sense. I just became Schwarz's pet not too long ago. Less than a couple of months now, I guess. I don't know any other pets. Do you have any suggestions on the best way to be a good pet?" Ansel is eager to keep her talking. She is beautiful and the thoughts are leaking out of his head as fast as possible.

"It is easy to be a good pet. Just be beautiful and obedient. It is also a good idea to be affectionate and kind to our masters. After all, it is by their will that we belong to them and belonging to them is the best," Ősz's tone in this explanation seems almost like something memorized and indoctrinated since birth.

If her mother was also Maestoso's pet, there was a very good chance that she was groomed to believe that she was not her own person, but rather simply a possession of Maestoso's to do with what he wants. Ansel is not so sure that he wants to really get to know her anymore or what it takes to be a good pet, but he really has nothing else to do.

"Oh, well, it sounds so easy when you say it like that. You don't do anything that you don't want to?" Ansel suddenly becomes very aware that Ősz has slowly been moving closer to him, watching him with intense interest that seems only too heavy. It is obvious what she wants, but it was equally obvious that they were in the middle of a field, in broad daylight, with their "masters" not ten feet away.

Ansel is daring, but not daring enough to be an exhibitionist. Plus he is not all that certain she is in her right mind and he is not into rape of any kind.

Even if she consents to sex, initiated even, if she really does not understand or think for herself, he feels he would be taking advantage of her, and that was practically the same as rape in his mind. He finds for every step she takes forward, he takes one backwards.

"Ősz, leave that poor boy alone," Maestoso breaks off his conversation with Schwarz to call to his pet. "Come and sit by my feet like a good little girl." He does not face her, and does not ask a second time before Ősz leaves Ansel's side and sits in front of Maestoso, leaning back against his front legs. "You really should not tease him. He really does not know that you are playing with him." Maestoso scolds Ősz. She does not look very chastened.

16

Chapter 16

Suddenly bereft of conversation, and flirting partner, Ansel settles himself on the ground and begins to read a book that he has brought with him for just this type of occasion. This book is a history of Germany, predating anything he has ever learned about in school. It was also written by someone who knew about the Magick creatures, and he detailed their roll in the guidance and creation of the various German tribes. It is an interesting book, if difficult to get through. The old German is not as easy to read as the modern German, for Ansel. *At least the subject is riveting. There is a lot here that clears up the various holes in our history.*

He might have been uncomfortable talking to Ösz, but he is sure he would have been able to explain it to her. Either way, she was called to her unicorn, so talking to her is out of the question. *Thinking about questions, I wonder if the myth that only virgins can ride unicorns is true or not.* Now, he is left to his own devices, hence the book. *Good thing I enjoy reading.* After all, even though he is incredibly excited to meet unicorns, he knew there was a good chance that he would be set aside to discuss various events that would not concern him and be left to his own.

"He is very well behaved for being such a new pet," Maestoso remarks to Schwarz, noticing how quietly Ansel is entertaining himself. "Have you considered breeding him? His temperament might make for some wonderful little ones. Plus his coloration and build would make for a stunning child, if paired with the right woman." Maestoso looks from Ansel to Ősz as he says this. He does not say that this is the match he might favor, but the implication is there. This makes Ansel's ears perk up and he begins paying very special attention to what is being said about him maybe making babies. The thought is absolutely horrifying.

It is not that Ansel does not like children, but he certainly does not want any of his own right now. Especially as he was still learning how to be a "pet" and is not fully convinced that this was where he wants his life to go, or if he would ever have the chance to be free again. He certainly is not willing to bring a child into his enslavement. And while Ősz is beautiful, and he would not mind spending the night with her, he wants it to be on her terms, not as part of a stud package through their masters. He just has to wait and see what Schwarz is going to say about all this, and then see if there is something he could do about the outcome if it is not what he wants.

"No, no, I really hadn't thought of studding him out. I don't particularly like children. They are a hassle to raise, always yelling and running around. I prefer to adopt my pets as adults, already trained on how to defecate in a chamber pot, or toilet now, I guess. Besides, there are so many of them. They are wholly over populated. Adoption, not breeding, is the way to go.

"I was actually considering maybe castrating him, like we used to do in the old days. They tend not to stray so much that way, not that this one has shown any inclination of straying," Schwarz answers, half satisfying Ansel's wishes, and completely horrifying him a moment later.

"Well, you know, they now have this thing called a vasectomy. It is like castration, but instead of removing the testicles, they snip some part of the anatomy making it impossible for the male to impregnate a female. It is supposedly harmless to the male, but it really doesn't seem to curb wandering, just the production of babies. It is also reversible if need be. I have it done to all the males that my pets produce," Maestoso uses the same tone of voice that one might use to discuss getting a dog fixed. Ansel all of a sudden knows how dogs and cats must feel under human "ownership." At least dogs and cats do not actually understand people languages or understand what is going on, he hopes.

"Schwarz, um, sorry to interrupt, but can we discuss what you just mentioned?" Ansel does not want this to be forgotten or assumed. There was no way he is going to be a eunuch for anything, death first. While getting a vasectomy would not be the worst, it was still more of a commitment than Ansel is willing to make at the moment.

"Yes, what is it?" Schwarz does not sound as though he minds being interrupted by his pet, despite talking to an old friend, who happens to be a unicorn. He turns to face a very pale Ansel.

"Um, if I promise to not stray and not make any babies, can I please keep my balls, not be castrated and not have to undergo a vasectomy? I really would not like either of those options. There are other ways to prevent babies and I have been very successful at avoiding getting anyone pregnant so far," Ansel is very anxious that Schwarz might not even consider his opinion on the matter, making it absolutely necessary for him to "stray," get lost and stay lost. He has enough money, he could find a way to get his family out of Germany and disappear. There were some things that he simply is not willing to do.

"I will consider this. Maybe, we'll see," Schwarz does not seem impressed with the concern that Ansel is displaying. Knowing that there was little else that he might do at the moment about this potential problem, Ansel settles back down on the ground to read and worry. All of this so he could go out and party for a night. He did not even get to go out, and yet he is still paying for it. Ansel has a feeling that he will be paying for that decision for the rest of his life.

17

Chapter 17

After a short while of talking in the meadow, Maestoso invites Schwarz and Ansel back to his stable for food and rest. Maestoso's stable is a stable in name only. In any other context, it could be considered a complex that itself is a study in beauty and luxury with multiple buildings and open fields and gardens built to delight all of the senses. In each of the buildings the ceilings were high, the rooms were huge, and the walls were covered in thick tapestries. The floors were an appealing mix of wood and bricks, with the bricks creating a pathway leading to various locations throughout the facilities.

It is during dinner that the next interesting part of the conversation came into being, the reason that no one came to rescue Schwarz in the forest for so long. After all, the distance between the forest and Maestoso's home was barely 4 hours away by car, no time at all over the past 200 years. It was hard for Ansel to believe that no one would step forth to help their friend out of his confinement.

Over a meal of rich meats, succulent vegetables, and a dessert of fresh fruit the conversation turns from pleasantries to politics of a magickal kind. That is not to say that Ansel does not have a hard enough time concentrating on what was being said. He has learned to expect many new things in his life, but learning that unicorns were carnivores was not one of them.

Ansel honestly thinks that the platter of meat arrayed on the table and served on the plate at the head of the table is for Schwarz. He is glad that he is not holding a glass or even a knife when he notices that it is Maestroso who takes that spot at the table. He has to force himself not to stare as the unicorn, who looks so much like a horse, proceeds to devour the served meat. Ansel had just assumed that they had the same dietary restrictions as horses. He is clearly mistaken. With extreme difficulty, he begins to focus on his own meal and the conversation going on at the head of the table.

"No one could go to your aid because of the elves and Easifat Ramlia. They held, and still hold, a true threat against your release. I have to assume if you don't already know this, that they do not yet know that you have escaped. Easifat Ramlia is still not yet over you besting him in flight over the deserts. He feels that he owns them and that you were an interloper looking to disrespect him," Maestoso sounds sorrowful at not being able to help Schwarz for so long and for being fearful of this dragon and the elves.

"Easifat Ramlia still has not forgotten about this? It was his suggestion to race the sands. It was hardly my fault that he didn't win, except that I did my best to win. Surely they all would have forgotten by now though, it has been centuries," Schwarz is taken aback that a single race might have caused so much trouble for everyone he knew. It might have been the Elves who imprisoned him for their own reasons, but Easifat Ramlia is the dragon who took advantage of this and terrified his friends into not helping him.

"Hardly, they regularly send representatives to remind us to avoid you, keep quiet and unseen. In this new age, there is not supposed to be any contact with humans, except for those that become our pets. The humans are now numerous, there is a very real fear that they might actually be able to defeat us," Maestoso shakes his head mournfully. He still remembers the dark Arabic djinn that had brought with him the instructions to stay quiet and not make waves less the wrath of Easifat Ramlia be brought against him.

The djinn that Easifat Ramlia sent to them was an Infrit. Infrits are easily one of the scariest of the djinn, but maybe not the most powerful. This one had plenty of power to spare, more than enough when his size and wings were taken into consideration as well. Infrits make great messengers being able to cross great distances with ease and even being able to be invisible to detection if they so wish, even to those who possess magic.

This one was red in coloration with large ram horns curled on his head. His wings were massive and he tended to flair them out while he talked. He was considerate, every time he came to remind them not to assist Schwarz. He was even-tempered and slow to take offense while being quick to forgive. He dressed in the most modern and fetching suit. If one didn't know better, someone could be forgiven for viewing him as harmless. That undoubtedly has worked in his favor in the past.

He delivered his message calmly, clearly, and with a minimal amount of wing flaring. He was the epitome of respect and almost seemed to be sorry he had to deliver such a threat to Maestoso. For their part, Maestoso and his family accepted the threats with the grim acceptance of the new restrictions being placed on them, knowing that there is nothing they can do about it. That the problem of Schwarz's confinement had resolved itself was of great relief to Maestoso.

"Come now, this is not the time for bad news. This is a day of celebration. Today is the first day that I have seen my dear friend, Schwarz since before Napoleon tried to take over a second time. Please, will you guys stay for a while? I am sure Ansel has not had much experience with unicorns. I'm sure he'd like to see our culture, learn about being a pet from pets, and maybe even learn something of the history of our peoples," Maestoso announces as Schwarz begins to darken with the threat of Easifat Ramlia. With an effort, Schwarz lightens up, focusing on enjoying the company and the opulence of Maestoso's home.

18

Chapter 18

With absolutely no fanfare, it is decided that Schwarz and Ansel would stay with Maestoso at his compound for a week on the inside and maybe longer if things go well. There is a lot that Ansel has to learn, and there is a lot of catching up for Schwarz to do. The world has changed a lot in 200 years. But first, they have to see the compound itself in all of its glory.

There are fields of beautiful light gray horses that fairly glow as though they are white. The few foals that could be seen are surprisingly dark, nearly black in color. These are the famous Lipizzans. These horses are bred with the interest of having fast, strong horses that could perform in a show and in actual combat. The unicorns occasionally cross-bred with them. The resulting foal would either be a unicorn, or a once in a lifetime type of horse.

There are several sets of stables, including a separate stable for mares with their foals or who are about to foal. The stables themselves feature herringbone design brick lining the walkways. Cushioned matting adorns the insides of the stalls themselves. Dark wood paneling with ornate iron fixtures is on each partition. The lighting is handled with brilliant chandeliers that are works of art themselves.

Each of the partitions is low enough that the horses next to each other can interact with if they so chose to. If they did not want to interact, there was still enough room that they did not have to if they did not wish to. Only the highest-end food is available, with enough variation to satisfy even the pickiest of eaters. And that is just for the horses.

The unicorns who live there each have open stalls that more closely resemble a bedroom than a stall. There are doors that they could close on their own for privacy, or leave open, which was the most common manner so that neighbors could visit as they chose. Each stall is painted to that unicorn's specific whim and decorated according to his or her personality. These specific barns are only accessible by an RFID keycard and all people coming in or out must be approved by the guard on station at the time.

This restriction is in place because there are so many humans on the campus at any given time, most of whom know nothing at all about the Unicorns. The campus is a riding school, so it would be unusual to find it denude of humans. It was declared long ago that humans could not know about the unicorns, but they still had to fund the farm, so this was the end result, security. It is there, to get Ansel his keycard and to be registered by the guards that they went first.

The next stop was the human dorms for those humans that the unicorns kept around them. These are just as luxurious as the barns, with no expense spared to provide for the comfort of those living on the campus. There are classrooms, daycare rooms, private rooms, and family rooms. The campus itself feels almost like a city to itself, providing just about everything a person would need to be successful.

The cafeteria is open twenty-four hours a day and is stocked with just about every food imaginable, with specific dinners being made daily. Today's dinner is Paella Valenciana and it is offered to everyone, no matter what time they eat their dinner. If they are not hungry for that, there is a wide variety of other foods that they can enjoy. The twenty-four-hour schedule is so that even those working nights on the compound could enjoy the hot, fresh food that those working day shifts can get.

Ansel is installed in an empty private room on the same floor as Ösz. She takes him to several of the classes about the history of people working in secret with the Magickal. The class is unironically called, Pets 101. It is one of those classes that runs non-stop. There Ansel learns that there have always been people who have been kept by magickal creatures. These people handle all of the day-to-day chores that creatures like unicorns and dragons simply could not do for themselves. He learns that these people are often referred to as pets because they so clearly mirrored how humans treated animals who were close to them.

He also learns that he has certain rights as a pet. He has the right to be happy, healthy, and safe. If he ever thinks that Schwarz is excessively threatening or that he was being abused as a pet, then he can call upon others in the community to petition for him. Unfortunately for him, threatening neutering or being kept locked up are not considered grounds for petition. He is also pretty sure that if Schwarz were to become physically abusive or actually wanted him dead, there would be no time for a petition to help.

He is surprised to discover that almost all of the humans that the unicorns keep have doctorate degrees in one field or another. They are often human medical doctors and veterinarians. Many have doctorates in farm management, economics, health care, and just about every other field available. There are even people with doctorates in history, religion, and literature.

He quickly regrets thinking that Ösz might be a little empty in the head when he discovers she is a psychiatrist specializing in behavioral mental health. He begins to feel really uneducated when she mentions in passing that she was currently studying for a second doctorate. He is a little annoyed to find that her earlier behavior was simply to get a rise out of him since he is so obviously new to the whole thing. *Hardly fair to take advantage of my ignorance about the situation that I find myself in.*

In the week that he and Schwarz stay, Ansel quickly discovers that he likes being around these people, Ösz in particular. He likes her charm, her quiet smiles, and her flirty nature. He likes the security of having a community that he can almost relate to, and that he is now a part of. A secret community that he would help keep safe by keeping silent about it. He also likes knowing that he could and should continue to take care of his family by demanding a salary from Schwarz, and telling them that it came from the Piber Stud farm in Austria. That would prevent them from trying to visit him and questioning where such a salary would come from. The last thing Ansel wants is for

Hannah to find him and get herself trapped like he is.

19

Chapter 19

I t is just another training day for Lukas Meyer. He does not particularly like training, but he loves being in the air. He would do just about anything to stay in the skies forever, even endure simple flying exercises. Granted, his Eurofighter Typhoon is rather an impressive way to touch the clouds, but it is almost impersonal. He is isolated from the skies in the heavy, fast plane in a way he is not in a small personal plane. He really does need to get his Ultralight back out and into the sky sometime soon.

Everything is looking normal for Lukas and his wingman Fuchs. They are just about to finish their 'little run,' as he calls it, and head back when out of nowhere, a huge shape emerges from the clouds. At first, Lukas thinks it is a weather balloon that got released without approval or notice, but no, it has wings and it is dark, not light-colored like most weather balloons. "Uhh... are you guys seeing this?" he calls through his radio. There is no way he is seeing a dragon.

"See what? There is nothing on the radar. You should have clear skies," the answer back is not encouraging. Nothing but him and Fuchs should be up here, and yet... Pulling out his phone, which he is not supposed to have with him, he quickly takes a short video and sends it to his commanding officer. He might get in trouble, but he rather doubted it. This is something they need to see.

"Sir, I just sent a video of what I am seeing. I have to assume that Fuchs is also seeing this," Lukas said as he thumbed the send button. He looked over at the other Typhoon, but he could not make anything out of Fuchs. He was nothing but cloth and a helmet to Lukas' eyes.

"What is that thing? And what is it carrying on its back?" The question was undoubtedly from their commanding officer. He must have taken over the communications station. Now to sound insane on a recorded line. With a sigh, Lukas begins.

"Sir, it appears to be a dragon. With a box on its back. The thing is huge. The dragon, not the box. The box looks like it could hold maybe a person or some small supplies, and nothing more. The dragon itself might be black or some dark green. It has a huge wing span and is making good time heading east," Yeah, he could be more specific and figure out the exact speed and heading, but he was not thinking particularly clearly at the moment. Besides, with it being an organic being, it could easily shift speed and direction, making all calculations worthless.

"Okay, observe the 'dragon' but do not engage unless absolutely necessary. I don't want to be the commander who ordered the death of the very last mythical creature in the world. I can just imagine how that would go. Nor do I want you to open fire and then come to find out that it is a kite. Just watch it."

With those orders, the boring training exercise becomes interesting again. Too bad they did not know exactly how interesting the orders would make their life. After all, what could possibly go wrong when you are tailing a dragon.

***

Since Schwarz had decided to stay for several weeks, with encouragement from Maestoso, he decides to show Ansel the sights from on high. They go up and are playing in the clouds, enjoying the sun on their backs and the freedom of the open skies. Well, at least until the skies are no longer empty. It seems as though one minute they are entering a cloud alone, and then the next, they are bursting out of the cloud with two Eurofighter Typhoons on their tail, quite literally.

Schwarz attempts to shake them, but the two planes stay on him, passing him every now and again to keep their speed up, but generally staying with him, no matter where he goes. In his frustration, Schwarz drops back, between the two planes, wings spread wide to slow his forward movement quickly. Unfortunately for the two planes, the reaction speed of the pilots was not as fast as Schwarz's movements, resulting in the short gray wings being clipped even shorter.

Schwarz hovers in the air, watching the two planes spiraling down to the ground with fire trailing behind them. He is shocked to see that the planes actually broke up rather than simply fold their wings and turn out of his way. It had not occurred to him that these planes that followed him were not living, but rather machines. The fact that there are people in those machines seems completely inconceivable.

It is not until Schwarz notices men ejecting from the two plummeting planes that he realizes what is going on. As the pilots are thrown from their planes, their parachutes deploy, slowing their descent to the ground. Not understanding parachutes, Schwarz dives towards the men, still strapped to their seats, and catches them, snapping their parachute lines in the process. The whole move took seconds, and in very short order they are all on the ground.

That is when the screaming starts. The men, even though they had seen the dragon from the cockpit of their planes, simply could not handle the concept that they were picked up and deposited to the ground by a dragon. A dragon wearing what looks like a cat carrier, with a man strapped in what appears to be a well-padded box. They scream. One of them manages to escape his seat and immediately pulls a small firearm from seemingly somewhere and begins shooting at Schwarz. Schwarz's response is rather underwhelming, moving only to be sure that Ansel is not hit by the bullets.

Once the pilot's firearm begins clicking empty, Schwarz attempts a dialog with the men. "Are you done now?" he asked the two men, one who is still stuck in his pilot's seat. This sets off a whole new set of screams as the men's brains try to process a talking dragon that apparently took no harm from a whole magazine's worth of bullets. Ansel tries the same line of conversation from astride Schwarz, but he does not get any response, their minds are still stuck on the dragon before them. Not that he is sure they even hear him over the commotion that they are making.

It takes a couple of more minutes before the pilots stop screaming. "Would you like me to take you back to wherever you belong?" Schwarz asks them, in a quiet and calming voice, much like the voice that one would ask a lost child where they last saw their mommy. Not trusting their voices, the men simply shake their heads, slowly.

"Are you going to be okay here?" Schwarz remains calm with them, not making any fast moves or attempting to approach them. He treats them like one would treat a lost puppy, and they respond in kind. They nod, again slowly.

"Well, this conversation has been enlightening, but I do think we should be going. Be safe!" Schwarz begins to back away from the men and once he has room and would not knock the men down, he launches himself into the air to head back to Maestoso's compound. As he takes off, one of the pilots pulls out his cell phone and takes a picture, sharing it on his social media account and setting a war into motion.

20

Chapter 20

As Schwarz approaches the compound, he notices a lot of commotion on the ground below him. There are people and horses, unicorns, and pets running from building to building, gathering supplies and securing padlocks. Walls that had not previously been visible go up, and defensive gates swing shut. Lookout stations are soon manned, and patrols can be seen in the distance. In a nearly empty field, a lone man is waving to Schwarz to show him where to land.

Once he alights on the ground, Maestoso bursts through the open doors of the palace, nearly frothing at the mouth in his anger. He begins screaming at Schwarz as he gallops toward the newly landed dragon. "Why?! Why would you do that? Didn't I just tell you that the magical creatures aree all staying out of sight? You are now news all over the world! You have been gone for barely 3 hours and you have managed to start a war! You just wait! There will be war!"

"Wait, what?" Schwarz is completely confused as to what Maestoso is talking about and how the world could possibly know about him, as he has only been in Germany and Austria for the past 200 years. Ansel had forgotten to tell him about how quickly news travels in this new world. He had not thought of it, after all, he grew up in this much smaller world with its near-instant communications.

Once Ansel dismounts, they follow Maestoso into the palace to see what he is talking about. "You have magic! You could not have hidden yourself and avoided a couple of fighter pilots? Were you trying to get caught? Didn't I mention that we were supposed to be hiding ourselves? You might be the stupidest of the dragons I've ever met." Maestoso is livid.

His unshod hooves clang in a manner that they should not be able to as he paces back and forth on the soft, wooden floor. There is a definite glow radiating from his horn, and it did not look wholesome or inviting. Instead, the horn radiates a bright white, almost blue light that chills the world in its icy brilliance. Schwarz proves he is mildly intelligent by not answering the unicorn in his irate state. Even the slightest sound might be enough to cause the unicorn to snap once again.

There, on the walls, apparently previously hidden by tapestries, are large television screens, turned to various news channels. All over the news channels are various images of Schwarz and Ansel flying over the skies of Austria, knocking down planes, and apparently catching and presumably eating the pilots of the planes. These images were taken on shaky cell phones and household cameras. Several of Maestoso's people are checking the social media pages from around the world. There is even a Facebook page about Schwarz already, several even, some calling to protect him, others calling to eliminate him. More pages go up in the few minutes that Ansel watches them work. He takes a step back, drawing closer to the dragon.

"I'd like to see them try to eliminate me. Don't they know that I am a magical creature? Their mundane instruments simply cannot hurt me. Swords bounce off, lances shatter, and arrows miss. Whatever that loud toy that the pilot was firing at me was, was nothing more than an annoyance on the eardrums," Schwarz announces clearly, in retaliation to the various reports of hunters gathering to run him down in Austria.

"No one uses lances, arrows, or swords anymore. They might not be able to hurt some of us magical creatures, but they sure as hell can burn down the forest, and our homes, and hurt our pets. Personally, I have managed to keep my horses and pets alive through a French invasion and two World Wars. I have no intention of losing them this time.

"I have not been discovered in centuries as anything but a white horse, and you have been free for a couple months at most and already you are causing me to potentially lose everything." Maestoso is furious. "You also seem to be forgetting that not all magical creatures have your invulnerability. Some creatures die easily at the hands of humans. It is those creatures you have put that the greatest risk." His mane flies behind him and his hooves stamp, denting the wood below him.

"Well, yes, that could happen. I am terribly sorry to bring this trouble down upon you. I will return to the Palace in the Mount, taking care to be seen moving away from you. That should help to keep the peace here. I really had no idea that information could travel so quickly in this day and age. The last time I flew the skies if a thousand people saw me, then it would take years before two thousand people would have heard about it. Apparently, news travels much faster now though," Schwarz's tone takes on the calm tone of someone who is thinking about their next move.

"Ansel, I am afraid that we will have to return home far sooner than we had anticipated. With Maestoso's permission, we can return once everything has calmed down. There is still much that you have to learn about your new life. However, we should definitely go home. We have a lot of preparations to complete. If there really is to be a war, we must make our home safe," Schwarz turns around and instructs Ansel to gather his stuff, and then heads out. Luckily for Ansel, he had not even begun to unpack, so it is in short order that they were in the air once again.

21

Chapter 21

To make sure to attract the most attention possible, Schwarz flies low over Vienna, flying between a couple of the buildings, ensuring that people would notice him. Then it is a race to Munich hoping to shake the attention before they make it to their own home, delaying the hordes that are certain to descend upon them. Schwarz is hoping that if he can go fast enough, with the right magics to make himself invisible, the humans would not even know where to start looking for him.

Once they are in the mountain, Schwarz drops the barricades, locking down the palace. The noise from the various barricades slamming in place shakes the mountain to its core. Ansel could not hear the people outside of the mountain, crawling all over to find them, but that did not make him any less nervous about them. After all, he knows they are there and they know he, or at least Schwarz, is there.

It took him a minute to figure out how people knew where to look, and it came down to the workers and the money that Ansel had been flashing around Munich. All of these people have likely told other people about the size of the place and the gold that has been flowing out of it. It really is not really that much of a stretch of the imagination that maybe the dragon seen in Vienna was actually living near Munich. It might have only been a couple hours since they were first seen, but news travels fast.

Ansel quickly finds several news reports with coverage of the mountain invasion, and the subsequent earthquake as the mountain became impenetrable. Apparently, half of Munich saw them fly over, despite Schwarz's magic, and are now crawling all over the mountain. Schwarz is sitting in the front room when Ansel finds him, surrounded by magic lights and darkness. He looks displeased. Apparently, the magic does not always work for all people and all devices. This was a hard lesson for the dragon.

"Did you know that news could spread as fast as light in this age?" Schwarz asks Ansel when they are both inside the mountain and sitting in the front room. His voice is low but does not sound dangerous. He just sounds resigned.

"Yes, I know that news can now travel as fast as light, or near enough to make no difference. I keep forgetting that you do not know these things. Otherwise, I would have mentioned it. Not that I think it would have made any type of a difference. No one could have predicted a pair of fighter planes being in the air at the same time we were. It is a shame that we broke them though. At least the pilots survived," Ansel tries to look on the positive side of the whole adventure. There is not a lot of positivity to be had about it though.

"Could you try to tell me when the current technology is going to give us trouble?" Schwarz does not want to sound accusatory towards Ansel. It is not his fault that they ended up in the situation that they have. No, Schwarz is experienced in the changing of time, he should have made sure that he knew the risks and did what he needed to do in order to mitigate them. It is not a pet's responsibility to take care of the dragon, but rather the other way around.

"I can try. Most of this is just natural for me though, I don't think about it. I don't think about the internet, instant communications, videos, or pictures. They've all just kinda been there most of my life. I will try though," and Ansel would. He might not be fully resigned to this life, but he can make the best of it while he lives it, and part of that would be helping Schwarz adjust.

"How bad is it?" Schwarz's voice is dark, concerned. Schwarz does not like all the people interrupting his life. He does not like that once again he is confined, and this time he could not even see the sky. He is trapped within a mountain unless he wants to cause more problems for the magical community. Plus, Schwarz knows that it will be only a matter of time before one of his crews pairs the palace and the dragon as one and the same, showing everyone the entrance, then the pounding would begin.

"It's bad, but the people are not organized, they are just wandering around and lost. They will lose interest shortly, call it all a hoax, and move on. Especially if there are no other sightings or there are a bunch of fake sightings, which is more likely," Ansel notes Schwarz's mood and tries to spin the news the best he can.

"Do you think?" Schwarz almost sounds slightly hopeful, but still concerned and upset.

"There was a dragon sighting in Dubai just a couple years ago, and even a dragon kill. When they released the video, it was obvious that it was completely fake. People will expect this to be fake."

"Well, everything looks better in the morning, so sleep sounds like the best move for now. Who knows what will happen by then," Ansel pats Schwarz on the leg, giving what little comfort that he can. Just because Schwarz is a dragon, bigger than an elephant, and he did kidnap Ansel from his former life, and ate Beno, doesn't mean that Ansel can't feel sympathy for him. Especially after that great week in Vienna.

With that, Ansel retires, leaving Schwarz to brood into the night and leaving strangers to wander on the mountain. Schwarz retires late into the night to toss and turn throughout the night, rising early and irritated. At least until he finds out that he has an army outside, ready to defend him.

22

Chapter 22

The morning finds Ansel once again watching the news channels and surfing on social media sites to see how much trouble they are in. The trouble seems to have taken on a whole new shape over the night, and he is not sure what to make of it. It turns out that PETA has turned out in numbers and is trying to force people off the mountain. They have blocked the roads onto the mountain and are patrolling for people who might climb up via one of the various paths. They have practically encircled the area in their protective glee of finding a new, and very rare, animal upon which to focus their lusts upon.

This is not the reaction that Ansel was really hoping for, but not one that he would lament. The PETA, People for the Ethical Treatment of Animals, people are absolutely crazy. He was hoping that all of this would just disappear and be forgotten about. He guesses that they left too much evidence behind, between the two destroyed planes and their low flight through Vienna.

With Schwarz's help, Ansel cracks a window and peered down the mountain, listening and looking at the area. He could hear the chants of the PETA people, but could not make out what they were saying. He could see the dust from the road, and assume it is from people blocking cars with their bodies. PETA is a crazy organization to begin with, and a dragon has apparently driven them insane. They have become the free army of the dragon, willing to protect them with all the zeal that they might muster.

"Do you think that they might think you're a vegetarian?" Ansel jokes with Schwarz as he watches them wander around, confronting anyone who tries to make their way up the mountain.

"Would it matter?" Schwarz does not know who or what PETA is.

"If they knew you ate a couple cows a day, it might matter. But, they do defend helpless lions, so maybe not." Ansel laughs at the image of a PETA member explaining to Schwarz that he should be a vegetarian. It is almost enough to bring tears to his eyes in this stressful moment.

"Helpless lions? Are lions actually no longer top predators in this age?" Schwarz is rather taken aback about that. Last he knew, while it was possible for a man to take on a lion, and win, the odds were pretty poor for the man, even if the man was armed.

"Well, yes and no. Lions are hunted, and poached, rather heavily for their body parts. It has greatly hurt the population. But, at the same time, the average lion is still a pretty formidable creature. There are hundreds of people injured by lions every year, and many of them are fatalities. The rest of them often leads to long-term disfigurement and disability," at least Ansel assumes that is accurate. He would have to google it later.

"And PETA prefers vegetarian creatures?" Who is this PETA and why are they so crazy, Schwarz is wondering. Why would the diet of one creature make it more valuable than the diet of another creature?

"Well, PETA does not believe that animals should be eaten. It does believe in wild creatures eating their normal foods, but they think that there is no ethical way to eat meat. They think that humans should not eat meat or animal products at all, including milk or eggs. They might be a little shocked to find out that you are a sentient being who eats meat, almost exclusively." Explaining PETA logic might be a tricky exercise, especially since Ansel does not really get it himself.

"And what does PETA stand for?"

"PETA stands for People for the Ethical Treatment of Animals. At least that is the official meaning of the acronym. However, a lot of people make fun of them by saying People for the Eating of Tasty Animals. They are considered a joke, or at least a bit crazy, by most people."

Thinking to make Schwarz relax and maybe even smile a bit, Ansel decides to bring up a topic that people have been speculating about since they first saw Schwarz, the box he was carrying. "You know my carrier? The one you were wearing on your back when we were spotted?"

Sighing, Schwarz answers him. "Yes, I know it very well. I had it made to my specific specifications."

"Well, apparently, people think it is a tracking device and that you belong to someone, not the other way around. They also think that someone might have been controlling you using the box." Ansel makes it sound like it could be plausible, much like the commentators on the internet are saying. He looks sideways at Schwarz, trying to gauge his response, hoping that the dragon would think it funny.

Luckily for Ansel, and most likely humanity in general, Schwarz does find it funny. He gives out s quiet little chuckle at the idea of anyone controlling him, especially from the box. "If only they knew."

After a time, in which neither Schwarz nor Ansel goes outside, the line between PETA and those hoping to slay, or at least get a picture of, the dragon is clearly drawn. There is yelling, picketing, and fighting along this line, on both sides and it is getting worse. The workers who have been going up and down the mountain roads to work only add to the confusion as they try to get up to the mountain to simply work.

PETA has tents up to provide shelter, food, and water, and they are not going to leave. The would-be dragon slayers could come to the mountain, but not up it because of PETA's blockades. They have no intention of leaving empty-handed, though. Some of them even begin breaking into what are clearly adventuring parties. Ansel could see the healer, tanks, and strategists building groups. If magic actually abounded in the human world, it would be Dungeons and Dragons come to life. The stand-off has begun.

23

Chapter 23

Ansel and Schwarz watch this drama unfold from the comfort of the palace. The chef has already been there, deciding that the cow he is preparing every day is for the dragon, and therefore he has been working for him for a while. With that decision in mind, he figures he would just keep working. There have been no cleaning crews in, but that is okay, the place is plenty clean as it is. Ansel is going to have to see if he can convince Schwarz to pay them anyway. He could clearly see them stuck behind the PETA barricade.

***

For Chance Goodteacher, it is a less-than-comfortable day. He is cold, wet, and tired. He had thought to come up to the mountain and defend it from trophy hunters, or at least that is what Iktomi said he had to do. He figured his time in the United States Army would come in useful, and it has. He is not dead, just dead tired. It has been over twenty years since he has been in the armed services, and it is telling.

He has been tracking this party of trophy hunters for a while now. Their tracks have become significantly more sloppy as they go, as though they are also flagging as they walk the seemingly hundreds of miles up this mountain. Chance is not particularly sure what he is going to do once he catches up to the party. Sure, he is armed with a couple of 9mm handguns, and he has his knives, but who only knew what they had. A gunfight might not turn out to be the best move he has made. He will have to wait and see what the next move brings him.

As he makes his way through the damp woods, Chance finally has a good look at the group he is following. Squatting down, he takes a good look at them. There are five men in the group. They are young, the same age as his kids, early twenties at the oldest. They also look like they are just ready to go home. What started out as a great adventure has ended in nothing more than a collection of blisters and being completely lost. Sure, they can get off the mountain by going downhill, but they could then land anywhere between one and a seemingly million miles from their cars. Chance knows how to handle this situation.

Taking a deep breath, Chance stands up and dusts himself off. He smooths back his long braid and straightens his shoulder pack. He is going to parent these kids out of here. Stepping out of the trees and into the clearing where the group is sitting, Chance smiles and says, "You guys look rough. Let's get you out of here," in the perfect German that Iktomi granted him when he helped save a dire wolf pup, leaving him stranded in Germany. But that's a whole other story and one that Chance is loath to think about.

"Who are you?" one of the young men asks. His dark brown eyes look bruised and tired. His hair is a mess, and his clothing is a testament to the number of times that he fell as he climbed the mountain. He appears to be the leader of this rag-tag group.

"I'm Chance Goodteacher," Chance answers back without thinking. Hum, that did not feel right in his mouth. Oh, that's right, Iktomi's "blessing." It translated his name automatically into "Risiko Guter Lehrer." With a deep breath, Chance tries again, focusing on the words he wants to say, his own name. As he does this, he once again begins to wonder why his first name translates differently every time. He gets it this time. *Yeah, that inspired all the confidence in the world*, he thinks to himself.

The youths must be more tired than they look because, despite the misstep with his own name, they nod and look like they are ready to follow him. He expected more resistance, to be honest. Before he gets them going though, he smiles, squatting down in front of them. *My knees will thank me for this later, I'm sure.* Reaching into his pack, he pulls out five bottles of water, one for each of the young men. Grabbing a sixth bottle, he drinks deeply and then finds some snacks to share. He has always thought that food went a long way to establishing trust, and these men need it.

Refreshed, they begin to follow Chance down the mountain. The way seems to almost open up for them, making it easy to travel through what is known to be a rough passage. "So, you told us your name, but that doesn't sound like a German name, and you don't look German, so who are you?" one of the men asks.

"Me? I told you, I'm Chance. I'm from Nebraska, in America. I belong to the Lakota tribe." At this Chance raises his left sleeve, showing off a medicine wheel tattoo. It is a series of circles with what appears to be a stylized sun connecting them. The circles are divided into four equal squares, each colored a different color. They are white, yellow, black and red. There is an expertly drawn spider in the center of the medicine wheel and four feathers surrounding it.

"You're a long way from home," another remarks.

Chance just nods to that. He could not be much further away from home if he tried. He still has to figure out how to get home. Every time he gets himself ahead financially, Iktomi would find a way to mess it up for him. *Tricksters, who needs them? Well, that really wasn't fair. The Dire Wolf definitely needed him, and Iktomi did help out almost as often as he caused problems. But, I really do miss my children and my farm. At least I can use Facebook to keep in touch with them.* "Tell me about it. I'll eventually get home again though."

The hike back is long, and they decide to stop after about an hour. They just need a small rest, catch their breath, and then they would continue. Chance luckily has a few more supplies in his bag since the five men ran out of supplies before he found them. As they sit and rest, Chance feels a bite on his tattoo. Rather than scratch at it, he stands up and begins looking around. Iktomi is present.

That is when he hears it, the low-pitched buzzing of a drone. With a smile, he greets the small, four-propeller drone that buzzed in front of his face like a bird. With a little wobble of a greeting, it waits for everyone to stand up before leading them slightly west of where they were initially heading, and down the mountain to safety.

Chapter 24

The unexpected event for the day, as far as Ansel and Schwarz are concerned, is when the German Military came in to remove both the would-be dragon slayers AND PETA. According to the German Military, neither group of people had the right to remain on the mountain, not when they were unsure as to what the disposition of the dragon is. There is simply too much risk that any people on the mountain might spark a territorial streak from the dragon, leading him to destroy the city below. Anyone who had watched the Desolation of Smaug would not like to see that happen in reality to Munich.

The Panzier Unit is quick to set up a new perimeter, off the mountain completely. They quickly surround all access points with wooden horses and post guards every few yards. The President of Germany announces on the news channels and declared that dragon hunting season is NOT going to happen and that if there is a dragon in the mountain, it can stay there, as it has obviously not been bothering people before. That they, and they alone, are going to investigate to determine the safety levels of having a dragon living in the mountain.

While this is easy to say, getting the dragon slayers and PETA off the mountain is something entirely different. The German military sends several Light Infantry units into the fray with orders not to kill unless actively attacked. Killing German civilians by the German Army would be a great way to cause more internal strife than simply having a dragon in a mountain could possibly cause. To achieve this, a huge number of soldiers are deployed. Many more than would have been deployed if the enemy were in the city and the rules of engagement were different.

Armored vehicles, such as the Boxer MRAV, are deployed and travel the newly paved roads on the mountain. Sporting 8 huge tires, there is very little area that they can not cover. Only the biggest of the trees could stop them if they decide to go through them. Their biggest obstacle is the mountain itself and the sometimes steep cliffs they would encounter. The fact that there are roads on the mountain helps quite a bit with getting them deployed, even if it did cause a lot of people to wonder why there are paved roads on the mountain. They finished clearing the dirt roads that criss-crossed the mountainside by their sheer weight. The sound of their heavily treaded wheels was enough to scare prey down the mountain, both human and animal alike.

Helicopters, such as the NHI NH90 TTH, a sleek transport helicopter, fly through the air, moving troops and prisoners alike. Its gray cameo print design makes it hard to see, even if the twin engines make it very loud. It is particularly effective at spotting people since the echoes off the mountain make identifying where the helicopter is nearly impossible and the people on the ground would often look up to the sky, making it easier to spot them.

German soldiers would often drop down from lines on the helicopter to break up fights between PETA and the Slayers, as they soon became called. It quickly becomes a game to the soldiers, with them keeping count of who manages to catch who and how many they were able to safely detain. Meanwhile, the PETA and Slayers are finding themselves with stories that they will be able to tell for years about how a soldier landed on them while they were out hunting a dragon.

It takes days to get everyone off the mountain. It is with the use of the MIKADO drone that the last pockets of the civilian population are found. The last group is a mixture of Slayers and PETA who had evidently found peace all on their own after a week of being alone in the mountain, separated from everyone else. The lack of food and water drove them together better than anything else could have possibly done.

Through all of this, casualties are surprisingly low. A couple of soldiers were injured through falls, a couple were injured while trying to apprehend different groups, and several civilians were injured trying to escape. By far, it was the PETA group that sustained the most injuries, mostly through fighting with the Slayers who were better armed in most cases.

25

Chapter 25

A few days into watching the battle, Schwarz remarks to Ansel that it might be a good idea to invite some of the politicians of Germany to visit him in the Palace to prevent any additional misunderstandings. There are obviously plenty of misunderstandings with the people at the moment. A misunderstanding with the government could be fatal.

With that, Ansel is on his way to Berlin. The hard part would be providing proof that he is a representative of the dragon, and not some random crazy person, pretending to have something to do with the dragon. A selfie is taken and Schwarz gives him a shed scale in hopes of that being enough. Ansel also photographs several ancient texts referring to Schwarz and images of him.

When Ansel drives down the road, he picks up his own escort and a plan. He finds the highest-ranking officer in the group, or at least the ones that can be spared, and returns back to the Palace. "Schwarz!! We have a guest!" Ansel shouts as he walks into the Palace with three military personnel in tow. He finds Schwarz in the great room, relaxing by the fire, and introduces his guests. They are three of the leaders in the 10th Panzer Division, Oberst Schmidt, Major Weber, and Hauptfeldwebel Schulz.

The meeting between the three military men and the dragon goes far better than the meeting with the pilots. Being prepared to experience the impossible, the men do not pull their firearms, or even express any disbelief. They simply stand there in shock for a moment, and then do their country proud by holding a civil discourse with Schwarz, resulting in several photos of themselves with the large dragon. It is after these pictures are taken that they opt to escort Ansel to Berlin.

As a testament to the quality of the references that Ansel gathered, and the seriousness that the German officials are taking Schwarz, there is barely a pause from getting out of the car with his escorts and sitting with the Federal Chancellor, Elisabeth Bauer.

Bauer looks like everyone's mother, hardly the most powerful woman in the world. Her blonde hair doesn't really show any gray and is cut in a bob. Her clean and modest and modern looks help to instill a sense of security and trust, even though you know you are dealing with an iron hand in a velvet glove.

"I hear you have a dragon," she starts with absolutely no preamble. She says it as though all of the introductions have been already made and that she already knows everything there is to know about Ansel. He thinks that she just might already know everything there is to know.

Slightly caught off guard, it takes Ansel a moment to answer. "Um, well, I don't have a dragon. Instead, he kinda has me. I'm not a captive, per se, but I kind of am his pet. Apparently, this is a common behavior with the mythological creatures in the world. They refer to themselves as Magicks." This is so not going as Ansel was planning, not that he really has much of a plan. Plus, he let on that there were other supernatural creatures out there. He will have to be more careful as this interview progresses.

Hopefully, she just thinks there are more dragons, but he has a sneaky suspicion that she will figure out that there was a lot more out there than just dragons. Either way, he is pretty sure that he was not supposed to mention that there are other Magick creatures out there, and he didn't want to admit that he was a pet, or a captive, or however they were going to take it. He has barely started, and he is certain that he's messed it all up.

"You're a dragon's pet," Bauer seems a little surprised, but her controlled features and postures make that a difficult read, so it really could mean anything. "I understand that these gentlemen with you also saw the dragon?"

How she got all this information without a call that Ansel saw simply astounded him.

"Um, yes ma'am," Is Ansel supposed to answer for them? He is so out of his element. Just a couple months ago he was chopping wood with Beno and now this. Yes, he had taken some classes while in Vienna, but not this advanced. He rather wishes Ösz was with him right now. She would know what to say or do. Maybe he should have driven to Austria first, and gotten some of Maestoso's people to act as diplomats with him. Hindsight is 20/20 and all. Is there a protocol for how to talk to Bauer? Oh, if he survives this, he is going to enroll in every class he can get a hold of.

It is Oberst Schmidt who steps forward and hands his phone over to Bauer, showing her the dragon and the pictures that they took with him. "He is a large, dark green dragon who appears to have human-level intelligence and self-awareness. While I am not qualified to discuss sentience, it does not appear that this creature is an animal, but rather a person. Schwarz, as he refers to himself, maintains a home in the mountains that is well-appointed and clean.

"Ansel lives with him and is free to come and go from what we were able to ascertain. While there is some threat to the public if provoked, Schwarz has testified to hundreds of years of non-violent existence before being discovered by the populace." Schmidt is clear and fast with the discussion of Schwarz's existence. He does a much better job than Ansel could have ever hoped to have done, in Ansel's opinion.

Bauer takes a moment and looks at the pictures of the dragon, several of which could be considered selfies with the dragon. She does not let on one thought as she considers them. The cut-throat world of politics has her better trained than any poker player. "Very interesting. What is your suggestion as a plan of action?"

Ansel answers faster than Schmidt, hoping to get the result that he knows Schwarz wants, "You and your cabinet are welcome to visit the Palace in the Mount at your convenience and meet with Schwarz. He eagerly awaits meeting you." His speech is a little stiff and sounds a bit awkward. He's nervous, none of this has gone as he expected it to. He is so screwing this up.

"And your suggestion, Schmidt?" Bauer says slowly, looking at Ansel the entire time. She clearly does not trust his opinion. After all, it wouldn't be the first time that someone tried to destroy the German government through some sort of a trap. This one would just be that much more elaborate than other traps.

"Ma'am, my suggestion is to hold off on military intervention until an attack takes place. Instead, send a small delegation to meet with the dragon and determine what it is that he wants and what it is that he needs. With luck, the dragon can be convinced to move to America or Russia, making him their problem," Schmidt says that last bit with a ghost of a smile. Just because the countries are "allies" doesn't mean that they are "friends." Even Bauer smiles a bit at that last little comment.

"Hum, that might be the best course. It is either that or engage in combat with an enemy whose defensive and offensive abilities are completely unknown. Not to mention that he could be incredibly rare and potentially valuable. If he really has been on our land for hundreds of years, I would be very interested to know why he has decided to come out of hiding now, of all times," Bauer is nearly speculative, but she still has the voice of confidence with her thoughts. Ansel is not about to admit to being the one who freed the dragon from his captivity, bringing him out into the open after all those years. "I will go and talk with Schwarz. I will take my assistant and Wolfgang Heinrich. He'd enjoy a dragon."

It takes the rest of the day to prepare, and they finally leave the next morning. It really is like going on vacation, it seemed like. There is a caravan of vehicles, tons of people, and packed lunches, and in the center of it, all is Ansel, being totally confused as to what he is supposed to do.

More than once he wishes he actually was able to learn more about his position from Ősz. He has a very short moment when he can meet Wolfgang Heinrich. He is an older man with a receding hairline and thin wire glasses. It is his eager smile that stood out the most to Ansel though. Heinrich is a man who is eager to meet a dragon.

They drive straight from Berlin to Munich without pause, and straight on to the Palace. Ansel leads them to the front door and lets them into the Palace, hoping that everything would be clean and orderly. A good first impression is high on his list of things that he wants for the day. Finding a cleaning woman in the front room running a cordless vacuum is not what he expected, but it could have been worse. It kind of makes the Dragon's lair, which is how Ansel is afraid that people would view Schwarz's home, appear rather domestic.

26

Chapter 26

It does not take long to find Schwarz. He is in the great room, posing before a large fire, listening to a young man playing the cello. Who this man is, Ansel has no idea. *Maybe one of the cleaners knew someone who could play the cello and called him in? If so, then how did he get past the blockade? So many questions and no time to ask them.* That Schwarz enjoys cello music should not have come as a surprise, but it was never mentioned before. Ansel gets the idea that this was set up by Schwarz to show his sophistication and culture to the guests. It came off as what it is, staged.

"Schwarz, we have guests," Ansel calls into the room, leading Bauer and Heinrich into the room, complete with all of their aids and personnel. Despite the number of people, there was more than enough room for everyone, and the Dragon, to feel comfortable. The sounds of the cello echo over the conversation, giving the whole room an almost eerie feeling.

"I can see that, Ansel. Who all do we have with us today?" Schwarz moves slowly and carefully around the newcomers. He doesn't want to scare them. He does not approach them. The cellist continues to play softly. The atmosphere moves from an eeriness to a warmth as conversation begins to flow and the music takes on the background sound, rather than the main focus.

"Well, we have the Chancellor of Germany, Elisabeth Bauer. We also have the President of Germany, Wolfgang Heinrich. They brought with them their aides and various other people whose names I unfortunately do not remember," Ansel has a feeling that he is screwing it up. *Ősz would have been smooth about this. She'd have known the proper ways to introduce everyone, their titles, and everyone's name. Heck, she'd have most likely made them all feel important and at home with a simple smile. I suck at this job, lifestyle, position, and whatever I'm doing anymore, I just know it.*

Turning around, Ansel addresses the crowd of people staring up at Schwarz, "And, um, this is Schwarz, the dragon."

Luckily, Bauer does not suck at her job. She approaches Schwarz with confidence and introduces herself, her staff, and Wolfgang with practiced ease. "Now, normally I have a dossier that tells me everything we need to talk about and what the specific protocols are for dealing with a foreign or domestic power. However, there simply is not a procedure written for dealing with dragons. We will have to rectify that. So, please overlook any rudeness as simple ignorance, and let us talk as friends and equals," Bauer's voice is light, belying the seriousness that she feels in this situation. After all, the whole idea that humans might be crunchy and go well with ketchup has not been unheard of by Bauer.

Schwarz smiles slightly, being careful not to show his teeth, and lowers his head slightly so that Bauer does not have to look straight above her to talk with him, "I'd love for that. We do not stand high on protocols here, as my friend Ansel has demonstrated." He glances over to Ansel, reassuring him that everything is alright and he did well enough with so little preparation and training. Ansel lets out a breath that he did not know he had been holding. After all, this could have gone so very wrong.

"So, what can the good country of Germany do for you?" Heinrich asks as he approaches Bauer's side, in front of the dragon. He looks like a kid in a candy shop. It has always been his secret hope to meet the fantastical, and here it is, a real dragon. The years seem to have lifted from him and joy fills his heart. Nothing like having a childhood fantasy come to life.

"Well, I and Ansel wish to continue living in our palace, here under the mountain, in peace. We wish to go where we need to go, without the risk of death or injury. We also wish for discretion, so that the 'media' as you call them, does not hound us at our door. I have managed for 200 years to stay out of sight, but that apparently has ended. Now, it is my hope that we fall back out of sight and continue our private lives," Schwarz answers the question directly. He almost misses the pleasantries and the bribing that various kings would do before any negotiations, but this is a new time and a new world. It appears that in this time, it is more common to be straightforward rather than circumspect.

"Well, unfortunately, we cannot monitor everything that our people do and communications have become almost instant in this world, so avoiding the media tends to be a bit of a difficulty. However, we can block the reporters from your home and provide you with as much privacy as possible. Now that the cat is out of the bag, there is no putting it back, there is only handling the situation as it stands," Bauer goes from the excited spectator look to the professional political leader that she is in a single second.

"First off, this mountain will become protected and private, keeping all those but those who have business here from being here. We will maintain a military presence until the heat cools off a bit. Then a statement that the dragon is a hoax and some sort of proof of that might be necessary. Maybe a large kite or something. That would lower the chances that others would post the sights of you," Heinrich interjects. He is not to be left out of this conversation.

Ansel has nothing productive to add, so he stays quiet and out of the way, watching how the entire conversation is being documented and recorded. Various people are recording the conversation by hand. Others are using recording devices, and even more are taking videos of the meeting. He marvels at the number of people who are being trusted to keep a dragon-sized secret.

Within an hour, all of Schwarz's needs are met. No requests are made of Schwarz besides that he does his best not to harm the peoples of Germany, an easy enough promise for Schwarz to make. After all, in 200 years, he's only killed one person, and that was in self-defense, kind of, and not something that Bauer or Heinrich need to know anything about. Pretty soon Schwarz is leading everyone on the same tour of the palace that he gave Ansel, except for the sleeping quarters and treasury. A banquet has been laid out for everyone to enjoy and feast upon. It is a truly wondrous experience and gives hints as to how leaders and kings dealt with each other in older times.

"I do have a question," Schwarz says as they are all enjoying a lavish dinner. "How is it that I have both the President and the Prime Minister in my home? Surely there is a security risk in having you both in the presence of a dragon. Suppose I was a feral creature, or that this had been a trap."

"I have to confess, that is my fault entirely. You see, Bauer was going to go with some aids and witnesses, leaving me behind as the sole head of government if it had been a trap. However, I would not stand for it. I have read every fantasy book I could get my hands on and have dreamed of meeting a dragon since I was but a child. I would not be left behind," Heinrich looks a little sheepish as he speaks. After all, here is a world power admitting that he likes fantasy books.

"While I could have backed down, and let Heinrich go alone, I simply could not give up the chance to see a dragon either. So, despite the considerable risk, we both went. It is poor tactics and high risk, but how many times do you get to introduce yourself to a dragon!" Bauer is rather animated as she speaks, now that she is in a less formal situation. The excitement felt by both of the visitors makes Schwarz feel hopeful about their relationship in the future.

Chapter 27

All too soon, the hall is empty of their guests and it is just Ansel and Schwarz once again. "That went well," Ansel hazards. He thinks through everything that could have gone wrong and is amazed that nothing major did go wrong. All it would have taken for the meeting to be an absolute disaster would have been for one person to have panicked and attacked Schwarz. Schwarz would not have hesitated to have eaten the attacker and then all bets would have been off. It would have been a full-scale war.

Schwarz takes a moment before answering him. "It went too well. I expected demands from me beyond keeping from eating the people. I do not believe that they will not come here at a later date, looking for my assistance in some matter. It has happened before."

"What do you mean?" Ansel has never heard of anywhere in history where a dragon was used, so he assumes it was as an advisor, although he thought that history should have mentioned something of working with the dragon. Although come to think of it, Ansel is pretty sure that world history has been altered to keep the Magickals out of the history books. Why else would no one remember them or be so shocked as to come storming up a mountain at the idea of a dragon.

"Well, there were the crusades and a few other military movements that the kings and religious leaders looked up to me for assistance. A dragon on a battlefield is a big morale booster for their troops and is very hard on the morale of their opponents. It was one of those engagements that I met Easifat Ramlia and how we managed to become such rivals," Schwarz sounds saddened at the mention of Easifat Ramlia as if what happened caused him real regret. Ansel gets the feeling that Schwarz is not yet up to discussing it. There is certainly a story there, but he can afford to be patient. All he has is time anymore.

"So, I should not be surprised if I find that I've been summoned by the German government at some time to solicit a favor from you for them?" Ansel is not excited about the prospect of another meeting with any of the officials that he has met so far. They all seem like they have a far better handle on everything than him and that with little work on their part, they would be getting him to agree to things that he would much rather not agree to. That could be why they are in politics and he was a farmer before becoming a dragon's pet. He is also surprised that Schwarz played so many active roles in world politics. It must have been a common thing for Magickals to participate in governments and interact with the lives of everyday people. Ansel almost feels bad that he was unable to grow up in a world like that, but at the same time, he rather wishes that he was not living that life right now.

"They will be nice about it, at first anyway. It will be small things. Like, can you get me to help inspire morale in their troops by doing a small fly-by. Or help train their personnel by showing them the different aerial maneuvers that I can do so that they can learn what they can expect to see at a later date from other dragons. Things like that. Things that appear harmless.

"But eventually those harmless things begin to take on more and more meaning. Soon it will be, could you follow the troops into a battle to reduce the morale of an enemy. Could you head a unit and protect them? Could you hold the heads of state in 'safety' until the governments can reach a peaceful agreement?"

The last sentence was said with the type of scorn that one could only obtain by having been asked to do that once before. Obviously, Schwarz feels that the last one is a breach of ethics. He is fine with "adopting" a "pet" but holding people hostage is too much for him, never mind the pet he has adopted is basically a hostage. The irony of the idea is not lost on Ansel. It was almost enough to make him laugh. The contradictions would have been lost on Schwarz.

"Either way, when they do finally come to you for favors from me, make sure that you continually inform them that you can take the requests to me, but that it is ultimately my decision. That should help prevent them from putting any undue pressure on you. Not that they won't try. While I'd like to think that bribery and blackmail are in the past, I rather doubt that human nature has changed that much in 200 years," Schwarz ends his statement with a yawn. While this has been exhausting for Ansel, it has been equally tiring for Schwarz. With that, they both head off to their separate rooms.

The next morning finds them with an entirely different set of problems. Ones that simply could not go away with time and a little diplomacy. Instead, it could possibly change the entire way that Schwarz and Ansel live and the entire path of Germany.

The next morning finds an Infrit sitting on their doorstep. Well, sitting would be the wrong term. He would never have been caught being so casual. He stands, erect and proud, awaiting someone to answer the door. His name is Rasul.

Rasul wears a deceptively expensive three-piece charcoal gray suit. It complements his dusky black skin tone and his copper-colored eyes. The ram's horns that curl over and then behind his head are an ebony black, polished so that they shine like onyx. The same can be said about his feet, cloven hooves that appear polished and clean. Behind him, sitting high on his back were a pair of dusty black wings that lay almost like a cape. All in all, he is the picture of elegance in a demonic kind of way.

Ansel is absolutely certain he was mistaken when he saw who was standing outside of the door via the monitoring systems that they had installed weeks ago. He is pretty certain that the coffee is drinking is not drugged, but who expects to see what he would consider a demon, standing outside his door. When the image did not change after a few minutes, he runs to get Schwarz. He would most likely know what to do with a devil at the door.

28

Chapter 28

While Schwarz and Ansel are busy dealing with an Ifrit at the door, another round of trouble is brewing in France, of all places. The trouble is brewing in a small coastal town that has the unopposing name of La Flotte. Not directly in the town, but further along the outskirts of that town, to be more precise. Hidden, in a palace that put all of the French palaces ever to shame, to be exact. This was a marvel of golden glory and light, manned by thousands of people, all living in the same little town. None of the residents are "pets," as they are kept by other Magickals. They are all employees, eager to work and please their dragon employers, both for the money and the safety of having a happy dragon.

200 years is not a long time for a dragon. It is barely a blink of an eye. 200-year-old grudges can easily renew themselves, especially if a certain dragon has managed to get himself spotted and bring to light that there is a whole world of Magickal creatures that most people did not remember existed.

Now, the time for open conflict and action is possible, and there were some creatures who feel that now was the best time to plot revenge. After all, it is always better to serve vengeance cold, and in 200 years, it has gotten ice cold.

For some dragons, this might just seem like the best time ever to settle old grudges and right some recent wrongs, at least in the way that they reckon time. This is exactly what Pluie feels. Now, now is the time to return Germany to France. Now is the time to avenge Napoleon. After all, if it were not for Napoleon, Germany would still be a series of tribes and clans battling against themselves. Granted, that was not Napoleon's initial goal with his Germanic neighbors, but that's what the results ended up being.

Then, once Germany rejoins France, all of the rest of the Napoleonic countries shall follow, giving his champion back the honors that he is due and rebuilding France into the EMPIRE that it should always have been. Besides, Germany needs to be punished for Martin Luther anyway. Who ever heard of nailing reformations to a door? What was wrong with the way things were. The Catholic Church was perfectly fine the way it was. Not to mention the downfall of the Holy Roman Empire could also be blamed on the German Princes.

Germany no longer had kings or crowned royals? Well, too bad for that. They would still suffer the wrath and vengeance that only a dragon of Pluie's caliber could bring upon them. After all, Napoleon was the champion that Pluie had backed and Pluie is never wrong about how the world should work under his rule. "Call up the French royals, it is time to go to war!"

Pluie is a little taken aback when he discovered that France was no longer a monarchy. King Louis the 16th was the last of the kings and he gave up his power in August of 1793. Time must have gotten away from Pluie. He seems to remember being angry about that at the time. He simply forgot about it though. It is just one more thing he'd lay at the German feet, if it was their fault or not. After all, why not.

Germany is to blame for just about everything wrong in the world anyway. Didn't they start the last two major wars, The Great War and World War II? Yes, there might have been something about an Austrian and some assassination, but Pluie was pretty sure that Germany was at fault either way. No? Well, the historians have it wrong, Pluie remembers, he was there after all.

No matter what though, how right or wrong Pluie's idea that everything is Germany's fault, he knows one thing for sure. Schwarz got himself seen. That means that all bets are off, as they say, and he can now act in the open. He will gather an army and march into Germany, taking it for his people. From there he will retake Austria, Prussia, and Poland. Prussia did not exist anymore either? Well, he'd take over whatever Prussia has become. He wants his Empire back.

While Pluie rants and raves over the prospect of being able to go to war against Germany, his lovely dragon mate, Papillon, watches him with exasperation. Pluie is always quick to anger and eager for battle. She, on the other hand, is far more interested in being pampered. She enjoys the peace that the Unseen Treaties have granted her. It gives her time to be polished, brushed, fed, and in general, relax. Schwarz getting himself seen and possibly putting an end to all of this is almost enough to rouse her from her relaxed state and go to war alongside Pluie just to ensure this doesn't happen again. Instead, she will try to mitigate it a bit.

"Pluie, darling, don't you think that you might be acting a bit dramatic?" Papillon calls from her favorite lounging spot. It is in a large ballroom with mirrors along one wall, catching the light. The mirrors have a light golden tint applied to their surface, giving the air in the room a golden haze feeling. She lays stretched out on the softest of satin pillows, basking in the sun. She is carefully arranged so that the light strikes her purple and orange dappled scales, setting them off in absolute glory. She hoped to distract her mate.

He spins around, looking at her incredulously. In the same light, the blue of his scales, tipped with a red so dark almost to look like blood, looked like a military uniform. He is striking. From head to tail, his scales may vary in size, but they do not vary in color or texture. It gives him a royal appearance that he took to heart from the moment he was a young hatchling all the way through to this moment. He is a king and the fact that the dragons do not have a king does not matter at all.

"I am not being dramatic. I am finally ready to act on the outrages that Germany has enacted against our people. They destroyed the Holy Roman Empire by forcing the church to sell the Ecclesiastical lands. All the work that Napoleon did to strengthen France and unite the Germanic Tribes, all of that was for not! It cost us a fortune to fund Napoleon. Plus the Holy Roman Empire was paying tribute to us. Now both of those are gone, and the German Princes are directly to blame for that. Not to mention all of the other horrors that I seem to remember coming from those lands.

"No, I am not being dramatic. I am finally acting on what I should have done centuries ago. I am finally going to take over those lands and bring the Germans to heel. I should have acted sooner, but I did not. I thought that the German people might be ready to rule themselves. They are not. Instead, they must now come home to us, begin to pay tribute again, and recognize the superiority of the French." Pluie believes what he says. He speaks with enough conviction that Papillon is almost convinced that this was not an ego trip. Almost, but not quite. She has known Pluie for a very long time.

"And where are we getting an army? There is no longer a king to frighten into submission. Now there is a Parliament and a President. You'd have to convince both of them that going to war against Germany was the correct thing to do. This is a government that does not even know you exist. What are you going to do, fly down to Paris and demand an audience? You might get one because you're a dragon, but that does not mean that they won't attempt to kill you or downplay your intelligence because you are not human. These people do not know you," Papillon says.

"I will fly down to Paris. I will demand an audience, and they will respect me both because I am a dragon and because I am more intelligent than all of them combined! That's final! Jean! Pierre! Gather the cars and some diplomats. We travel to Paris!" The last bit is called loudly to the two heads of the palace. These are the individuals who would help to ensure that the palace itself runs smoothly.

Jean Martin is a tall but spare man. At 50, he is experienced in just about every situation that comes up in the palace. He, like most people in La Flotte, has lived most of his life in service of the dragons and has actually spent most of his life in the palace proper. His graying hair is never out of place and his suit fits him like a second skin. He is almost a match to Pierre Simon who is 25 and is dressed in the same suit, but his hair has yet to lighten from its natural black with any hint of gray. Pierre is second in the palace and set up to follow in Jean's footsteps. There is almost no time before they find the appropriate people and set up an impressive caravan.

As these two competent men rush about to handle the logistics of moving a huge mass of people to a site just outside of Paris, Papillon tries one more time to calm her enraged mate. "Now, what about Schwarz, have you taken him into account? He is now free of his curse. You know, as well as I do, that he does not fancy himself a ruler, but he does have some tendency to come to Germany's aid." Papillon remembers the last time that Pluie met the devilish rogue, Schwarz. It did not end well for Pluie.

"What does Schwarz have to do with it? If he feels he must get in the way of avenging Napoleon, then have it be on his head. I will defeat him like I did last time. It is not like he could have gotten any better in the interim. He was trapped in a hovel, in the middle of nowhere. How he ever escaped will be forever beyond me, but he might as well have just stayed there." Pluie puffs his chest out as he speaks. His recollection of his last meeting with Schwarz is apparently not the same as the one that Papillon has.

"Hum..." is all that Papillon is willing to comment after that.

29

Chapter 29

While there is always a functioning government in France, that does not mean that they are always functioning in the Parliament building or that the president is always home. After all, these are busy people who are trying to balance the needs of a country, as well as their own lives. It should not be surprising that the Parliament is not open on a Sunday, but days do not register like that to a dragon.

In Pluie's mind, everyone should be ready to receive him at a moment's notice, no matter that it has been a couple hundred years since he's actually made an appearance. Not that he is actually at the Parliament himself, instead he has sent a trusted servant and was less than thrilled to find that person returning to their encampment with nothing to show for it. This does not surprise anyone but the dragons, but who is going to tell them that they are wrong, especially Pluie.

Instead, Pierre Simon takes it upon himself to look up and find the information for the President of the National Assembly, or at least her secretary, and let him know that he has a very pressing matter that he needs to handle immediately. Upon learning that this pressing matter is a dragon who is looking to invade Germany, Antoine Laurent, secretary to the president is immediately contacted and makes his way to the camp where Pluie and Papillon are. And that is how France manages to avoid having Paris sacked by an irritated dragon.

The encampment that is set up for Pluie and Papillon looks nothing like a modern encampment. The tents are not small pup tents of a dull gray or green. All of the tents are of bright, loud colors that invite observation, rather than hiding from it. The largest of these tents, and the brightest with banners flying high on them were the ones that the dragons slept in. The layout is not in strict rows and while there is order, it is order of a more fantastical nature than a military nature. Tents are laid out in a circular pattern around the two large center tents, Pluie's and Papillon's, obviously.

The first ring of tents, closest to the dragons, are the special advisors and management staff that serve the dragons directly. This includes Pierre Simon, his group of assistants, the various diplomats, and favored pets. The second set of tents are the various helpers who traveled to Paris with them. This includes people who handle the food, the people who handle the tents, and people who keep everything clean. Even the lowest of the tents are well cared for, clean, and bright. There is no need for guards. Only an idiot would attack or steal from a Dragon.

Laurent arrives quickly, as well as his guards and various officials. It does not take him long to find the encampment. A large encampment of over fifty brightly colored tents is shockingly easy to find when it sits on the outskirts of Paris. Not that Pierre left it to chance. He is exact with his directions on how to find them. He does not want to be the one who manages to get Paris burnt to cinders. That does not mean Laurent could actually agree to what Pluie is planning.

"You want to... invade... Germany. To set up the Holy Roman Empire... again," Laurent stammers after hearing Pluie's plan. His sense of disbelief in the very notion of invading Germany is dwarfed only by the fact that it is a dragon who is telling him what the plan is. The whole thing seriously makes him question exactly what mushrooms were on that pizza he ate. He had never been so glad to be just the secretary and not the President.

"Yes, and it will not only be Germany. We must retake Prussia, or what was once Prussia. Napoleon did the job once, and we will redo it since the entire thing was brought down into ruin due to those German princes. The Holy Roman Empire must rise from the ashes and re-establish itself as a powerhouse." Pluie bellows that last part, as though volume is enough to make the whole thing take shape.

Laurent simply stares up at Pluie, in shock at what he is hearing. There is no way that his plan is going to come to pass, but there is an equal chance that he is not going to be the one to tell the dragon that. Nope. That job would most definitely fall to someone else. Someone who is NOT directly in front of the dragon. Laurent has some phone calls to make.

"Okay, well, unfortunately in today's society, there is a lot to be done to get an army ready to move. We no longer house all of the soldiers in a single location. Instead, they are scattered throughout France. Let me talk to the military leaders, and the president of France, and we'll get this ball rolling. Gotta re-establish Prussia, too. Otherwise, we're just taking pieces from other sovereign nations.

"I'll have to make some phone calls, do some rearranging. How about we get back together on this later this week." As a way out, Laurent is rather proud of himself. He promised nothing, and he still might be able to get out alive. Then he will bump this up the ladder so someone else can handle it. Mythical, fantasy creatures are not something he signed up for.

Pluie considers this for a moment, then nods in approval. This quick jerk of the massive dragon's head in Laurent's direction is startling. Laurent found himself jumping back suddenly, nearly tripping on the uneven ground. He haa done it. He haa managed to get himself out of this deadly situation, and he is going to go home and change out of the wet slacks he is wearing. Everything is going to be alright. He just has to convince the President of France that he's not insane, that he really did talk to a dragon about invading Germany, their strongest ally.

30

Chapter 30

It would have been alright if Pluie had forgotten about the entire idea of invading Germany like he had so many other plans. Instead, he remains camped just outside of Paris, awaiting a response from the President of France. Pretty soon, Pluie begins to realize that the Paris government is not taking his demands seriously. Do they not realize that he is a dragon? Do they know that they are in positions of power upon his sufferance? It is time to remind them. Paris might not burn, but it would definitely stand up and take notice of Pluie.

Papillon does her best to calm his rage. She primps and preens to get his notice. She flatters and charms to calm him down. It dulls the tip of his anger and takes the flames from his speech. He would not go and level the French government for not heeding him. He would talk with them. It had been a long time since they had to follow his guidance, they simply did not know that he was to be answered to.

At that, on a Tuesday, a day that he was certain that the government would be in session. A day that Pierre has gone ahead and verified that the heads of state would be in residence, Pluie makes his modern-day debut in the busy city known as Paris. He flies low through the city, knocking people down, stopping traffic, and leaving his entourage behind him. His descent onto the lawn of the Palais Du Luxembourg is impressive. It shakes the building to its foundation. His bellow for attention could be heard on the other side of the city.

The response he receives is not the one he is hoping for. Instead of the President and the Prime Minister rushing out of the building to do his bidding, he is surrounded by soldiers. Instead of being treated as a benevolent ruler, he is treated as a hostile entity. He is enraged. He is further enraged when they open fire with their weapons, as though they thought that they might prove effective against a dragon. His scream of frustration shatters the windows in all of the surrounding buildings.

It is then that Papillon makes her appearance. She lands lightly upon the ground next to her life partner, glancing over at him as though pitying his lack of patience with the humans. Once the gunfire has dissipated, in absolutely perfect formal French, Papillon asks to see the heads of state. The fact that she could speak, and speak their language, is more than most of the people in that courtyard can handle. They stand there, dumbfounded. "Please?" and with that the spell is broken and someone runs back into the building.

When Camille Dupont, the President of France, comes out to greet the dragons, she does it with the calm assurance that there is nothing she can not handle. In her early sixties, she is healthy and fit. Her short, silvered hair is immaculately styled. Her bright blue eyes quickly move over the scene, taking everything in, including the two dragons on her lawn.

She walks with the self-assurance of one who is certain that there is not an emergency that she cannot handle. That's not to say she is stupid in her confidence. She wears what armor she could quickly acquire. It might only be a Kevlar vest, but her clothing itself is bulletproof and supposedly fire-resistant. She is pretty sure it was not dragon-tested, but for the price she paid for her clothes, they might have been.

Dupont proudly stands before the dragon pair, gazing at them in a bit of wonder, before asking, "What is it that I can do for you two, today?"

"Finally, someone who has their head on straight," Papillon sighs.

"We must go to war! We must retake Germany and re-establish the Holy Roman Empire as it once was. Napoleon did the work once, and we must see to his that his sacrifices for his country are not forgotten and his progress lost. We must mobilize the armies immediately. I have dallied too long as it is, and it is imperative that no more time is wasted. To arms!" Pluie announces, stepping forward as he speaks. He soon pushes Dupont back into her people. He stands there once finished, face turned to the sky, and does not see the look of absolute confused astonishment on Dupont's face.

"Well, we can't very well just go to war with Germany. We are allies. We are one of their closest allies in all of Europe. It would be a betrayal of trust to simply attack them, even with the intention of re-establishing the Holy Roman Empire. In addition, if we were to attack Germany, we would see heavy sanctions from the United Nations. It could easily cripple our own country, as you attempt to make it stronger," Dupont answers, calmly. She is thinking fast. She is fairly certain she is not going to be able to talk this dragon out of trying to force an altercation with Germany. *Maybe delay him? What happens if I simply say no to this whole crazy scheme? Do I then get eaten? Of course, this would happen during my term.*

"Good sir, I am very sorry, but I don't think I ever got a name to which I may address you," Dupont adds after her denial to the dragon. Maybe if she could establish a report with the being, the situation could be smoothed over. Especially since from the corner of her eyes, she can see the press forming a ring around them all. She could hope that they wouldn't be able to hear what was going on, but with the volume of the dragon, she is absolutely certain that this was all going to be on the international news just as fast as they could send it.

"You do not know who I or my partner are?" The tone of outrage is undeniable in Pluie's voice, even distorted as it is by the sheer volume. "Have you forgotten who truly rules these lands? Have you forgotten at whose sufferance you hold your own title? Have the traditions of this fine land been so watered down over time that the dragons have been forgotten?!"

"Pluie, dear, it has been almost 200 years since we have graced them with our presence. And ever since the treaty, most of the society has become nothing more than mythologies to these people. You must give them a little bit of leeway for forgetting their places. But, we are here now, so we shall take back our roles, and lead this country to the glories that it once was," Papillon interjects. She can see clearly that Pluie is close to simply eating the woman who stands before him, even as he needs the woman in order to accomplish his own goals.

Pluie turns his blue head towards Papillon and gazes at her for a solid minute before turning back to Dupont. He seems to have regained his composure after gazing at the Butterfly of the Dragons. "I am Pluie. I set up this country before the whole idea of France ever came to be. I have guided its rulers for hundreds of years. I have funded some of the greatest ventures that this land has ever seen. Napoleon was my champion. I funded his military actions and guided him through his successes. It is now time to renew my investment into these lands and reclaim those that were once mine."

"Pluie? Rain? I am Camille Dupont, President of France. The Prime Minister is currently out of the office, else she would be here as well." A lie, as both women would never confront a potential enemy at the same time. There is no reason to place the stability of France at that much of a risk.

"Please forgive me, but I have not previously heard of your involvement with the governance of France. I have not even heard a myth of your existence. That being said, I can hardly deny that you stand before me. With that, let us adjourn and reconvene in a week with a plan on how to handle the German problem. Simply marching into the nation may not be the best way to handle it at this time. Especially with how much France has to lose." With that Dupont bows forward, awaiting some form of acknowledgment that Pluie agrees with this request.

"One week. That is acceptable. We shall meet here, in a week's time. At that time, I expect the armies to be arrayed and ready to march forward onto Germany. I will not be swayed otherwise. I will reign total destruction upon these lands if my will is not heeded," Pluie announces, staring directly down upon Dupont. After several minutes of watching Dupont not falter, despite the obvious fear of all those around her, Pluie jumps into the skies, and with several strong beats of his wings he is away.

"Do not doubt him," Papillon tells Dupont in a quiet voice. She sounds almost saddened by the idea of war and destruction. "He may love France, but he does not enjoy his will being tested. If he is not satisfied with the results next week, he will destroy Paris, and all of its surrounding lands, simply to get his point across. If his will is still not done, then the path of destruction will continue until you agree to do all that he demands." With those final words, she takes to the air with all of the grace one could scarcely imagine from such a large beast.

Once the two dragons are out of sight, Dupont marches back into the building. "Get the German Chancellor on the phone, immediately. We have to figure out how to invade Germany without actually invading Germany." For once, Dupont looks like she might not have everything under control.

Chapter 31

"And, as you can see, even though you are not a signer on the Unseen Treaties, you are still under the edict. You cannot allow yourself to be seen, and having done such, you will have to be fined. The fine itself is determined by the amount of damage done to the community at large and the disruption caused by the sighting.

"A small fairy being caught in an English garden will garner a much smaller fine than, say, hitting two fighter planes and causing a small-scale battle on a mountain. Not to mention getting posted on several worldwide news programs, Facebook, and various other platforms. The extent of the damage done by this incident requires a heavy fine. I do believe that the agreed-upon fine by the council and treasurer is 30,000 gold pieces." Rasul looks almost pained to inform them that the fine was going to be that huge. Not that he likes handing down punishments to those who had not even been informed of the Treaty. He always felt that some form of lee-way should be given to those who could not have known. But, he is certainly not in charge.

"And who, pray tell, is on this counsel?" Schwarz knows better than to eat the messenger, but he is sorely tempted. Although an Ifrit of Rasul's standing could be a rather difficult meal, one that could possibly bite back.

"The council has several members of each of the various species of what the humans refer to as mythological and we refer to as Magickals. For the dragons, Easifat Ramlia is your representative. He is the one who decides how heavy the fines should be and if there should be any lee-way in how to handle the situation. He also collects the taxes from each of the dragons every decade to ensure the smooth running of the council. That tithe is the meager amount of one hundred gold every decade. That being said, he has asked to inform you that you are behind in your taxes. A bill will be sent regarding that amount." Rasul knows of the animosity between Schwarz and Easifat Ramlia. He does not expect the idea of paying taxes to him to go over well. He inwardly winces at the torrent he is expecting.

"No. We will not be doing that. There will be no taxes and no fines. You have discharged your duty and informed me. You may deliver whatever paperwork is required. You may take whatever token of proof that you have discharged your duty that is necessary, but you will not take a single gold coin from this house. I will not take my wrath out on you, but if Easifat Ramlia wants my gold, he will have to come and take it himself." Schwarz could have frozen the ocean with the ice in his voice.

Ansel is watching all of this with interest from his spot off to the side of the meeting. They are all in a fairly large study. Well, it is decidedly not feeling all that large now with an irritated dragon and an Ifrit who is attempting to remain cool in his presence. The old texts lining the wall and the comfortable fireplace was making this room feel rather like a tinderbox as tensions were getting higher.

This is the second day that Rasul was in their home. The first day they treated him as a guest and put him in a well-appointed room to allow him to relax after his travels. He took his dinner in his room and Ansel did not have much of a chance to interact with him. Today, Ansel had led him to this study and found him to be polite and interested. Under other circumstances, Ansel is pretty sure he would have liked Rasul.

Rasul had spent several hours going over the Unseen Treaties. He has several scrolls and one codex that he used to explain the entire thing to them. He even has a copy for Schwarz, although in human size. In these treaties between the Magickals, no individual is supposed to be seen by the humans at large. There are clauses in the treaty for individual humans, or families of humans who have been previously tied to the Magickal world. There are even procedures for when humans call upon or actively seek out the creatures. Schwarz is in violation of a lot of clauses.

"You and I both know that there is no doubt that Easifat Ramlia will come here to take what he is due. He will likely increase that amount, leaving you a beggar in your own mountain. I do highly suggest that you give him his due." Rasul does not like the idea of leading an army to Schwarz's door, and he is pretty sure that is what this is going to lead to.

Schwarz scoffs at the idea of Easifat Ramlia coming to his door to collect some taxes. Taxes are such a human concept. "Let him come. I've defeated him before, and I will do so again if necessary. I don't know how he got the other dragons to agree to this human notion of taxes, but he will not see even a copper from me. Not even so much as a Euro. No, I am afraid you will have to leave here unsatisfied and return to your masters empty-handed."

"If there is to be no resolution, I will take my leave of you then. Thank you for your hospitality. You have been a gratuitous host." Rasul stands at the end of that sentence, apparently ready to depart immediately. Ansel is a little surprised by this. He expected the debate to go on longer and become more insistent. There were not even any raised voices. Apparently Rasul knew of Schwarz well enough to know when his mind was made up and to give up on his attempt.

"Ansel and I will walk out with you," Schwarz indicates to the door once Rasul has gathered his paperwork. He leaves the copy of the treaty that is for Schwarz on the table but takes with him the intricate scrolls and codex.

"Might I have a shed scale as proof that I have indeed spoken to you in regards to the treaty?" Rasul hates to ask, but if he returns to Easifat Ramlia with no gold and no proof that he discharged his duties, there is a potential for harm to himself. While he could handle himself well against most creatures, dragons can be very dangerous. He would rather just give proof, rather than take the risk.

"It might not be enough to satisfy Easifat Ramlia that you have completed your task, but yes, I will grant you that. If he does decide that you are to be punished, you may return here for sanctuary. I enjoy your presence and would be honored to assure your safety," Schwarz answers Rasul. Turning to

Ansel, "Please grab a shed from the treasury. Try to find the best example in the room."

Ansel quickly hurries down the hall to the treasury. Shed scales are not common, but they are not uncommon either. They were simply a part of living life for the dragons. These are scales that have become damaged or worn and then fall off, kind of like shed hair. But, they are often used as proof that someone is in the employ of a dragon, so the shed scales that are in good condition, with the bright colors of the dragon, are often kept.

Ansel had long ago organized the sheds that he kept for situations like this, not that he had actually expected anything at all like this. He had expected to have to give them to humans as proof or bribery to get what they needed. Either way, because he had organized them, he is quickly able to find a large, but manageable green scale to give to the Ifrit. Soon he is heading back the way he came from to help walk out the demon on his doorstep.

32

Chapter 32

Ansel is rather glad to have Rasul leaving. Yes, Rasul is the perfect house guest. He has been quiet, and respectful. He gave out bad news, but he did it without being threatening. It just is, nothing he can do about it. He is but the messenger. Nothing more. That does not mean that Ansel is not glad to have the Palace in the Mount to himself and Schwarz again. He dislikes the idea of a stranger being in his home.

At least this is what he is thinking as he runs into the foyer. He sees Schwarz and Rasul finishing their discussion as he approaches. He can not make out what they say, but he does not miss the motion from Schwarz for him to open the door. As soon as he reaches it, the doorbell rings with a crystal clear note. It stops Ansel in his tracks.

"Who else did you happen to annoy, my dear Schwarz?" Rasul teases. He casts a sly look over at the dragon, fully prepared to take the credit or to sidestep the blame, depending upon what was behind that door.

"Who I did, or did not annoy is hardly your concern, Rasul. Please, take the shed and know that your task has been completed." Schwarz is beginning to get annoyed with all the surprises that this era seems to have brought with it. First instant communications and machines in the skies. Then armies of people appear on his mountain. Now an Ifrit telling him to pay his taxes. This last surprise is just a little too much. Who knew he would ever miss that cabin in the woods.

"Go on, answer the door, Ansel." Schwarz's voice has just a hint of a growl in it. Whoever is on the other side of that door had better have a good excuse for being there.

Handing the shed scale to Rasul, Ansel turns back to the door just in time to hear the chime ring again. "Impatient..." he mutters as he reaches for the door's knob. He no sooner opens it, than he slams it shut again, bracing his back to the door. Nope, Ansel would rather deal with a dragon and an ifrit than what is on the other side of that door. There are few things more terrifying than what he saw there. Matter of fact, he could only think of one thing off the top of his head and that would be his mother.

"ANSEL!!" screaming can be heard from the other side of the door. The voice is high-pitched, young, and full of rage. The type of rage that only a sibling could impart. The type of rage that lets you know that they will hurt you in ways you can only imagine because you have lived with them for your entire life. It is the scream of the oldest sibling at her younger sibling.

Both Schwarz and Rasul stare at Ansel as he takes deep, terrified breaths and leans against the door. They have seen all kinds of human behavior, but this is a first. They do not know Hannah. They only saw a young, furious woman and now a terrified man. "Who is that?" Schwarz says softly. No need to further terrify his pet. If this is what he thinks it is, Ansel is in a lot of trouble. If this is what he thinks it is, he would definitely be getting a hold of Maestoso's human doctor.

"That is Hannah. That is my older sister. That woman is going to kill me, then ask questions, and then likely kill me again." Ansel's eyes are wild and wild. He flinches when Hannah screams his name again. He can not quite make out what else she is saying, but his name definitely has the ring of murder attached to it.

"Invite her in, sit her down in the study we were just in, and get her some wine. I will see Rasul out. We have too much to do for you to simply stand there and block the door. Not to mention that it sounds like she is not going anywhere," Schwarz calmly instructs. Maybe Maestose had it right in breeding the right humans. This one seems to be defective.

"Right, yeah, bribe her with wine. Maybe see if we have chocolate. Books, she can be bought with books. I might survive." Ansel seems to be talking to himself. He nods, this time clearly to himself, and takes a deep breath. Straightening his back and squaring his shoulders, he opens the door once again.

"Hannah! How nice to see my favorite sister!" Ansel does not have time to invite Hannah in. She simply grabs him by the front of his shirt and pulls him towards her car. Ansel can not resist her and finds himself being dragged behind her like an errant child. *When did she become so strong? Or did he just get weaker, not having to do the physical work that he used to do on the farm?*

"Humans. They have such drama that we look simply boring in comparison," Rasul comments to Schwarz as they step out into the afternoon light.

"To live with every emotion to be acted upon must simply be exhausting. I do hope she doesn't kill Ansel. He was finally getting the hang of his new life, and she looks like she'd be more work than it is worth to keep." Schwarz sighs.

"Good luck. And with that, I'm off." Rasul leaps into the air, clearing himself before flourishing his wings, and pushing himself higher into the sky. Soon he is out of sight and on his way home to report to Easifat Ramlia.

33

Chapter 33

" I have a job in Munich! I work for a rich person, doing procurement. Here, let me send you all kinds of money in a sketchy-ass bank account where all of the deposits are cash," Hannah mocks Ansel. She has him trapped. He is up against her car and she stands between him and the entrance of the Palace in the Mount. He might be able to knock her down and make a run for it, but he is pretty sure that she would make him suffer if she even thinks that he thought about it.

"Well, in a way, that's all true. We're just out of Munich and I do all of my shopping and banking there. I do procure things for Schwarz. He is rich." Ansel hunches into himself as he answers her. He is instinctively protecting his vital organs from his enraged sister. He might be bigger than her, but his body and spirit know that she dominates him.

"Right. Because it certainly does not look like you were running drugs or had gotten caught up in some cartel or drug ring. Mom was not absolutely certain that you were laundering money through the farm, thinking you would not be caught that way. She hasn't been worried sick for you for the past few months, no, not her. Not at all. You and Beno have been known to do some wildly stupid things, but this one takes the cake," Hannah shouts back sharply. The last word is punctuated with a quick jab, knocking Ansel lightly against the car. It is not enough to hurt him, but it is enough to ensure that he is still paying attention to her.

"You don't understand. And I can't explain it unless you promise to actually listen. Why don't you come inside, I'll get you some food and wine, and we'll talk. No bullshit. Nothing but the absolute truth," Ansel answers quietly. Everything Hannah had said is true. He could feel it in his soul. The bit about Beno hurt though. He had not thought of his friend much since his death, and to be reminded of him was almost enough to break him. Hannah could see the pain, even if she does not know why her brother hurts.

"Fine. I'll listen," Hannah relents. She takes a step back and allows him to lead her into his new home. The dragon she had glimpsed, and the demon she thought she had seen are nowhere in evidence as she steps through the darkened portal.

Ansel leads Hannah, not to the study as Schwarz suggested, but rather to the second kitchen. This is Ansel's kitchen. It is nowhere near as well set up as the main kitchen. The highest-end item in it is either the refrigerator or the espresso machine. But it is Ansel's. He feels comfortable there and he figures Hannah might, as well. Especially, since like every family he has ever known, they did not hang out in the living room, or the library, or any other room except the kitchen. All important conversations happen there, around a plate of food and a mug of coffee.

Hannah sits impatiently at the heavy oak table that Ansel had dragged in weeks ago to eat his favorite snacks at. It was similar, if a better quality, to the one that is on the farm. It even has the small drawer in the middle that he loved so much when he was younger. Instead of sitting down, Ansel crosses over to the refrigerator and starts getting out food to cook. He is going to make Jaeger Schnitzel, not quite from scratch. The chief prepped most of the ingredients, so all Ansel has to do is combine and heat them.

"So, how is mom?" Ansel decides to tell Hannah the news that Beno is dead after they eat. The same goes for all of the details about his current life. He'd let Hannah talk first.

"Oh, she's worried about her ONLY son. It's all that she has talked about for the past few months, how you and Beno are likely working on getting yourselves killed, or worse. She won't even touch the money that you keep putting in the checking account. It just keeps building, and I keep falling behind on the chores, but we can't hire anyone to help because she is certain you're going to need the money to pay back whatever wild debts you're digging for yourself.

"Every time there is a new car on the street, she is certain it is some gangster looking for you. She has me stop whatever I'm doing to come inside with her. As if someone who is looking for you, with intent, would be hindered by a simple wooden door. As if there is not a huge picture window facing the back fields.

"On the plus side, she is at least over her obsession with the woods. She has declared that the evil that was lurking there has gone from the area. Now I can harvest wood close to home. That is literally the only thing that has gotten easier since you left. And now, I find you in the company of a demon and a dragon. Mom is going to have a cow." Hannah started her rundown of Mom, leaning forward over the table, but ended it by throwing herself against the back of the chair she is sitting on. It was a well-built chair and did not so much as creak.

Ansel, on the other hand, listens to the rant standing straight at first and ends it hunched over the simmering pot of hunter gravy that he is heating up. He can hear Hannah's frustration and the worry she has for their mother. He can feel the concern she has for him, and the irritation mixed with relief of finding him whole and well, if with unsavory company.

"You have been doing all of the chores on the farm? You have had no help?" Ansel is a little surprised about that. He knows Hannah is a strong woman, but there is a lot that needs to be done on a farm, even a small one. He is pretty certain he would not be able to manage it all on his own.

"Well, not quite all alone. I've had some help," Hannah's voice takes on an embarrassed note as she makes that little confession. Ansel turns around to look at her and sees her face turn a rosy shade of pink.

"Oh? Inquiring minds must know." That is Hannah's favorite phrase. She would appreciate Ansel using it.

"He's just a friend. His name is Otto. I met him at the library when I was returning Dragon's Ring. He was returning the second book in the series. We got talking, and he came up to the farm to visit. And you know how Mom is, she took one look at the guy sitting at her table and put him to work. Surprisingly, he keeps coming back. He's there right now, taking care of things for me while I'm here."

"A friend... who willingly works on the farm... most likely for free... for you. You have a ... unique... view of friendship. Will you only be dating when he asks for marriage? Might consider him a significant other once you have a couple kids with him?" Ansel has to tease his sister. It is the law of being a sibling. If he didn't, some being is likely to swoop down and steal his "Little Brother" card.

"Shut up, brat," Hannah spits, but without the venom that would make it sting. She is smiling, happily thinking of Otto. *Oh, she has it good.*

Ansel checks on the pork deems it cooked, and plates the food. Setting it down, he grabs silverware and a craft of coffee. Now to tell her about his life.

34

Chapter 34

"First off, Beno. He did not lead me to this. He did not cause this. This was all my fault, and I got Beno killed. It was my fault. I should have listened to Mom. She said not to go into the woods, and Beno and I wanted to go out, so we decided to fell a small tree in the woods, at night, to get enough wood so that we could go out that night. I knew it was stupid. I did it anyway, and it got Beno killed.

"He died at the jaws of Schwarz, immediately after I broke the curse that kept him in those woods. I did not break that curse intentionally, but I did it nonetheless. Schwarz appeared to us as a young woman, and we believed him. When he transformed, Beno attacked him. Beno paid for that with his life. I was then taken into captivity by Schwarz to be his "pet." I cannot get out of this without risking him destroying the farm and all of you.

"I set up the checking account with the money that he gives me to buy myself things and the "wage" he gives me for being his pet. There are actually other "pets" in the world, and they have a kind of union where they protect each other and help ensure that some rights are given to those who are "pets". I met some of them in Vienna, in the service of unicorns, of all things.

"I have to stay here. I have to follow his rules. I cannot leave without permission. I am left to do my own thing most of the time, but if he needs me, I have to respond. It keeps you guys safe. It keeps me safe, as well. I am hoping that in time he either gets bored and lets me go, or he gives me permission to go home and visit you guys," Ansel explains, not quite to Hannah, but rather to his plate. He does not look up to her until he is finished, his eyes red with unshed tears. He has not given himself time to grieve for Beno. He has not given himself time to miss his family.

Hannah grabs Ansel's hand as she listens to him relate everything that happened, especially with Beno. Beno was like a second little brother to her. She grew up with him as Ansel's best friend and constant companion. He was always over. And now, he is gone and had been gone for months without her knowing about it. Tears spring to her eyes as she thinks about him.

"Oh, Ansel. Why didn't you say something when you call? You should not have had to go through all that alone. You have a family, a family that you can always rely upon." Hannah feels as though she has let her little brother down, even though there was no way for her to have known where he was or that he needed her help. Big sisters are always supposed to just know when their baby brothers need them.

"I didn't want to worry you. I didn't want you to rush down here and put yourself at risk. I was trying to protect you," Ansel's voice breaks as he answers her. He has failed at both of those tasks, and he really missed his sister. He really misses his mom.

Taking a deep breath, Hannah makes a decision. "I'm calling mom."

"What? NO!" Ansel is horrified about that prospect. His mom would come down, and get herself killed going after Schwarz. Or get all of them killed, or somehow manage to start a war and get everyone killed. Their mother never did things by halves.

"Relax. I'm not going to tell her about Schwarz. But I do need to tell her that you're safe and not under the influence of some weird cartel or gangsters. I don't know what I'm going to tell her about Beno, but she deserves to know that you are safe. There is no way that I'm going to tell her that you're being held hostage by a dragon. I'm not stupid," Hannah assures Ansel as she flips her cell phone from her pocket to her hand. She always had a great sense of coordination.

Selecting their mom's landline, Hannah quickly tells their mom that Ansel is safe and that she was right, he is in Munich. Hannah does not let her mom talk beyond answering the phone. She promises to call back soon and be safe. Ansel just stares at her in awe.

"You did not even let Mom get a word in edgewise." That is a neat trick. He would have to remember that one, talk fast, and not stop until hanging up. No wonder Hannah was always in less trouble than him. She never gave mom a chance to yell at her.

"Nope. And by the time I call back, I'll have a better story for her. One that won't end up with a dragon burning down Germany or her attacking your dragon. I know our mom. I have seen her take on scarier things than a dragon."

"Like what?" Ansel could not think of much that was scarier than a dragon, at least in his life before Schwarz.

"The tax man. The Tegernsee Counsel. You know, people who think too highly of themselves and feel that it is their right to tell widows what to do with their lives and their children." Hannah is of the firm belief that while there are apparently monsters in the world, humans are still most likely the worst ones. She might be right.

"How did you find me, by the way? I did not exactly advertise that I am being kept by a dragon, or that there really is a dragon just outside of Munich. Not that I'm not glad you found me, but still." Ansel had done his best to stay out of the sight of the media, or so he thought. He did not talk to reporters, and the German government swore that they would not be releasing any information on him or Schwarz. He believed them when they said that, only because of the public reactions when they were first spotted.

"Remember when Schwarz hit those planes in Austria? Well, video footage of that was released all over the place. There were a couple seconds where you were out in the clear, talking to the pilots before Schwarz stepped in front of you. Just a glimpse. But I could spot you anywhere, even from behind a dragon. I'm your sister, after all.

"Then there was a weird battle here. I quickly put two and two together, got four, and decided that you had to be here. It just took me some time to convince Mom and Otto to let me go and get you back. Otto insisted that it should be him, right up until I pointed out that you have no idea who he is and that he could not identify you in a lineup to save his life. Mom said it should be her because she's your mom. I put an end to that one by reminding her that she's old and that it could be a long walk up the mountain.

"Finding the right road took me some time. But then I noticed that there seemed to be a car driving up and down the mountain at about the same time every day. I assumed it was you, although it seems to have been your cleaning crew. I got to know them when I pulled in next to them and started demanding answers. They seem nice." Of course, Hannah figured things out in the most illogical method possible, while still being right. There was no direct line between any of the points, but she still made it work for her. She should have been the pet, she'd actually know what she was doing in political situations.

"Well, now that you know what is going on, at least in the general sense, why don't I show you around and get you a room. No sense in you staying at a hotel in Munich when I have tons of room here that you can use," Ansel says as he finishes his dish, slaps his thighs, and stands up. He gathers their plates, depositing them into the sink to take care of later.

Hannah thinks about arguing with Ansel about it but decides that she could argue later if she decides she does not like the offered rooms. If she did, then she would stay with Ansel and cancel her hotel room. She had packed her bags in her car in case she needed to make an escape, so she did not need to return to Munich at all if she was staying here. Instead, she just stands and follows Ansel out the door.

Ansel knows his sister. He knows what she would like the most and what she would be apathetic about. He could have shown her the gaming room he set up for himself or the theater room. He skips those completely. Instead, he takes her to the library. As they pass the doors to the various rooms, Ansel does define what each room is, but he does not open all of the doors. He points out the heavy detail work on all of the doors and lintels, knowing that it was something that Hannah has always been interested in.

Finally, they make it to the library where Ansel pauses, holding the door closed for a moment, building up the anticipation levels. With a flourish, he opens the door for Hannah and watches her face as it goes from reserved to open wonder in a matter of moments.

Hannah falls immediately in love with the library with its shelves upon shelves of ancient texts. Most of the books were well over 200 years old, preserved in pristine condition thanks to Schwarz's magic. The rest of the books are ones that Ansel picked up for himself. While Ansel was not a heavy reader while at the farm, he did reacquaint himself with the pastime now that he no longer has to spend most of his days working on the farm. Hannah is definitely staying the night in the Palace in the Mount.

Hannah decides to spend a week with her brother. Her first few meetings with Schwarz are a little tense. She views him as the captor, a kidnapper, of her brother, and he views himself as Ansel's adoptor. They eventually decide that simply rehashing the same disagreement about Ansel's status is unhelpful. Soon it became a process of negotiations between the two. Hannah wants Ansel to come home and stay home. Schwarz has no plans on letting Ansel leave for any extended period.

All of that came to a halt three days after Hannah arrived when Bauer showed up with a train of assistants and personnel in her wake. War is coming to Germany and she needs Schwarz to put a stop to it.

35

Chapter 35

I t is bright and early when Bauer rings the door chimes on the front door. Ansel and Hannah are enjoying a breakfast of poached eggs that was made by the chief when they hear the bell. They look over at each other, and both hope the same thing, that it is not their Mom. She might not know where they were exactly, but they don't doubt that she could track them down if she wanted to. She has that knack.

Wiping his mouth and standing up, Ansel sets off for the security room to see who is at the door. He motions to Hannah that she should continue her breakfast, but just as he expects, his oldest sister follows him. If it is their Mom, he is going to need backup. Instead, he finds the German Prime Minister at the door, waiting none too patiently.

It is only a scant moment before Ansel takes off towards the door to open it for Bauer and her entourage. He leaves them in the large formal room and takes off to get Schwarz. This leaves Hannah with the head of her country to entertain. She tries her best not to look like a deer caught in headlights.

"You are Hannah, right? Ansel's older sister?" Bauer asks Hannah, even though she clearly knows the answer.

"Uh, yeah," *Right Hannah, try not to sound like an idiot in front of the Prime Minister.* "Yes, I'm Ansel's older sister. I just arrived a few days ago." Hannah assumes that Bauer knows everything about their family, having had to deal with Ansel. Undoubtedly, there is someone who was watching over their family, in case they ever need to "persuade" Ansel or Schwarz into something, not that Schwarz has shown any interest in their family, just Ansel.

"How have you been? Your mother is well? Are you handling the farm alright?" Hannah is certain that Bauer does not mean for the questions to sound threatening and creepy, but to Hannah's suddenly stressed mind, they are terrifying inquiries. This woman knows everything about her, it seems. She would be happier when Ansel arrives with Schwarz to get the attention off of her.

"Everyone is good, I mean well. The farm itself is hard work, but we're managing. I'm hoping to get Ansel back to the farm in time to help with the planting that will be coming up," Hannah quickly answers. She has no idea where to go in the conversation.

"If not, I am sure that there are some people who would be happy to help you out," Bauer smiles at the end of the statement. Again, Hannah is certain it was not meant to be creepy or threatening, but she sure feels that it is. Could Hannah look forward to finding government contractors "helping" at her farm this upcoming spring? She rather hoped not.

Luckily for Hannah, it was just that moment when Schwarz comes striding through the oversized doors with Ansel following behind him. "To what do I owe the pleasure of hosting the Prime Minister in my home?" Schwarz sounds like this is indeed anything but a pleasure.

Hannah is rather glad when Bauer turns to face Schwarz, seemingly to have forgotten about her. She is even more glad when Ansel appears at her side and leads her to the side of the room. She is eager to see what all of this is about, but not quite so eager to not wish it to be done already. There is a lot of pressure being in the same room as Bauer, even if she is not the center of attention.

"I am afraid we need your help if we are to avoid a major war." Bauer does not engage in any type of pleasantries or attempt to sidestep the problem. "My counterpart in France has called me and informed me that they are required to invade Germany in hopes of re-establishing the Holy Roman Empire for an individual who goes by the name of Pluie. They, and we, are hoping that you will be able to stop this from happening. Do you happen to know this dragon?

Will you be willing to attempt to save our nations?"

"Pluie? The Holy Roman Empire? Tell me that old fool is not still harping on the German Princes and Napoleon. France is going along with this? What exactly are you hoping for me to do about this?" Schwarz responds incredulously. He might be able to handle Pluie, but the entire French military might be a bit much. They might not be able to injure him, but that doesn't mean they couldn't hurt him or make a general nuisance of themselves.

"The current plan is that we allow them to enter our country and 'take over' some previously cleared towns. Meet them once they cross over and have you handle Pluie, who will be traveling with them. It is our hope, and France's hope, that not a single shot needs to be fired and that no one is injured in this process. The French government does not want war with Germany, but they also do not want Paris and the surrounding areas destroyed by an upset dragon, as he is threatening to do."

"So a mock battle, no fatalities, between your armies, and then I handle Pluie. I'm going to assume you don't want any collateral damage or losses, right? It is supposed to be all neat and clean, without any fuss? Is that what you're picturing?"

"Well, we were hoping to avoid even the mock battle. We were not going to field any military resistance if possible. Just let them walk in and then have you handle Pluie. The French military is not even going to carry live ammunition. We are picturing a play battle, a fake invasion, nothing remotely real. We understand if in handling Pluie buildings get damaged. We are prepared for that. We do not want to have people injured though, if possible. Buildings can be rebuilt. Most of them have been rebuilt. People cannot be."

Schwarz thinks about this for a second. It could work. Well, almost. If Pluie thinks that they are getting one over on him, he will destroy Paris and attack the German towns just out of spite. There will have to be modifications to this plan. Something to make it look far more real. "All of this could work, but it won't. You are forgetting that you have to fool Pluie into thinking that the invasion is real. If you have France waltz right into an empty village, Pluie will notice. He will also notice if there is no responding German army. He is not stupid. Well, he's stupid, but not that stupid."

"What do you suggest?" Bauer was right, Schwarz apparently knows Pluie and how Pluie would think and react. The best part, it sounds like Schwarz is actually going to help them.

"I'm going to suggest that you populate the town with actors or military personnel. Keeping the civilians out of the way is important. Then you're going to need to field a military reaction to the French military. It does not need to be huge and no one needs to carry live ammunition. They just have to look and act like they are. Then have everyone scatter once I land to handle Pluie. If I'm lucky, I can keep it on the ground and prevent it from becoming a fatal battle. We will need room. Oh, and make sure everyone is wearing waterproof gear," Schwarz looks like he is beginning to have fun with planning this mock battle. Bauer wishes she was having as much fun.

"Waterproof gear?" Bauer asked. Everything else sounds like it makes sense, right up until that. This far out, over a couple weeks away from the mock invasion, Bauer could not be sure what the weather was supposed to be. Schwarz does not even pretend to check the weather or ask when this was happening. What did he know that she didn't?

"Oh, you'll see." Schwarz smiles in anticipation.

36

Chapter 36

As the delegations continue between Bauer and Schwarz, figuring out the timeline for the invasion and the various details, Hannah turns to her brother. "Is this your life now? Meeting with government leaders and saving the world?" she whispers. She does not want to interrupt the conversation going on in front of her or attract any attention from those in charge.

"I would love to say that this is not the norm, but this is the second time in two months that I have met Bauer. I have also met Heinrich. And we had a battle of sorts on this very mountain not too long ago. I'm sure you heard about it." Ansel answers back, a little meekly. He ducks his head and rubs at the back of his neck in embarrassment. He never liked to get a lot of attention from authority figures, and now he seems to be up to his armpits with them.

"So, the answer is yes. This is your new normal," Hannah deadpans. "Big difference between running around with Beno and avoiding responsibilities to this."

"Yeah... I kinda feel that I'm going to need help. And training or something. I am so out of my league," Ansel laughs. Before Schwarz "adopted" him, Ansel barely knew who the heads of the German government were, let alone be able to pick them from a lineup. Now, he feels that he could almost call Bauer by her first name and get away with it, almost.

"Well, if this dragon is anything like the ones in the fantasy stories, he should be able to afford a private college for you. If you decided not to go with the public colleges," Hannah always felt that Ansel would do well in college, provided he was able to keep it in his pants, something he'd never have been able to do with Beno around.

"Well, there are resources that I can use, as well as traditional college, as a 'pet.' There are people in Vienna who take care of Unicorns, and they have classes that they run all year long that touch on situations like this. I might have to get a hold of them and see if I can do an online class or something." Ansel had forgotten that he failed to mention that he met unicorns to Hannah. Or rather he had, but it was only in passing, she most likely missed it.

Hannah turns slowly to her younger brother. He might be taller than her, stronger than her, and backed by a dragon, but he met unicorns and not only did he not insist on getting her so she could see them, but he did not even tell her. He is a dead man standing. "You met unicorns?" Hannah's voice is menacing and icy.

Ansel takes a side step away from Hannah. He might be bigger. He might be stronger. He still fears his older sister. She could still kick his ass, and he knows it. With wide, terrified eyes, Ansel tells her the truth. "Yes, and we stayed with them for a week. That's what we were doing when we were spotted in Vienna with the planes. We had been visiting with the Unicorns." Ansel is going to regret this, but he has to say it now before it comes out later. "And we saw the Lippazan horses. I even got to ride some of them."

Ansel is trying to stay quiet, while still avoiding Hannah. It isn't going well and some of the aids that Bauer had brought with her are getting irritated with their discussion. The siblings are getting silent glares from people who were busily taking notes as to what was going to happen between France and Germany. When Hannah swings to slap Ansel's shoulder, one of the aids has seen enough. She hands her notebook to her neighbor and roughly grabs Hannah's arm to lead her out of the room.

The next thing that happened occurred so fast that most people were unsure how it came to be. One moment a woman had grabbed Hannah's arm and was reaching for Ansel, and the next thing they all knew there was a dragon standing between the siblings and the same woman. People were on the ground, some groaning in pain and shock, others staring around confused.

"I will help you guys avoid a war. I will even engage Pluie. I will not tolerate anyone laying a hand on my people. Hannah is Ansel's sister. That makes her one of mine. The next time anyone touches them without permission, for any reason, they will answer to me. There will be no third time. Is that understood?" The last sentence was not actually a question. He is staring down the woman who had acted so rashly. His voice deafens her, sending goosebumps of fear through everyone standing there. Hannah and Ansel stand behind him, shaken.

"Ye... Yes. My apologizes. I will never touch those under your protection again," she stammers. A wet stain appears on the brown skirt she is wearing. She has peed herself in fear. Schwarz growls one more time at her, showing her the impressive teeth that gleamed so brightly next to his dark green scales, before backing up half a step so she could scramble up and away from him. Not that she could actually get away if he decides to eat her.

Bauer, tough as always, and loyal to her people, steps forward, between the aid and Schwarz. "She did not mean it in a manner to harm your charges. She was simply trying to keep them from distracting the rest of the group. She will know better than to try such a thing again. Please. Let her get up and clean herself off. She is very afraid and has most certainly learned her lesson." Bauer stands with her hands apart and at her side. Her posture all but screams that she is in charge and willing to take responsibility for the mistake.

The turning point is when Hannah comes forward, between Schwarz and the aid and assists the woman herself. Hannah steps up and helps the woman stand, brushing dirt off her. "Ansel, which room?"

That is all Ansel needs to snap out of his shocked stupor. He brushes past Schwarz like he is the family cat, and leads the way to a well-appointed bathroom. "This way. I'll show you to the guest bathroom. I unfortunately don't think any of my clothes will fit you. I have a laundry though," Ansel offers.

"I think I have a skirt or something that will fit. I'll grab it from my bag." With that, the brother and sister team manage to defuse a situation in which

Germany could have lost an ally, ended up actually having to fight a war with France, and Schwarz would have lost standing with his host nation. Not that they could evict him, but Germany could certainly have made it more difficult to stay there.

It is no time at all before the aid was back in the room, freshly washed, dressed, and even fed. In that short interval, Schwarz and Bauer had set up a timeline and formalized plans on how to pull off a deception against a dragon. For the sake of two nations, and possibly the world, it has to work. The downside, it is definitely going to go against the Unseen Treaty that Rasul had just talked to them about. Well, Pluie could just pay the fine.

Chapter 37

Ansel immediately starts to pack once Bauer and her aids leave. He runs around, gathering clothing and various things that he feels he would need for an extended journey. It is only after running around for half an hour that he realizes he has no idea what he is going to need to go into battle. He would have to talk to Schwarz.

Ansel expects to see Schwarz preparing himself to go into battle. He is not sure what he expects, maybe to see Schwarz strapping on dragon-sized plate metal or something. He is not expecting to find the great dragon lounging in front of the fireplace, taking a nap. He does not expect to find Hannah sitting next to him, using him as a backrest as she reads a book. He does not expect the tray of cookies that are next to her. *Where did they get cookies?*

"Gathering flies?" Hannah asks as he stands there, shocked at the lack of concern being displayed before him. *Did they not realize that they were going into war, or at least mock war, in order to prevent a larger war? Did they not take this seriously? Am I taking this too seriously? Why didn't this come with a manual? Would I have read it if it did? At this point, I'd read anything if it meant understanding what the hell was going on.*

"Um, I thought we would be getting ready for battle, not lounging around. Did I misunderstand something? Are we not battling Pluie for Germany?" Ansel is so lost.

Hannah looks up at him. His wide brown eyes and his disheveled hair making her think of when he was a little boy, lost and confused as to everything that was going on. Especially when they lost their father, and he suddenly found that he had responsibilities and was being called, "The Man of the House." Oh, how she felt so bad for him back then. Now, this Ansel just makes her want to laugh.

"Oh, brother of mine, how long do you think it will take to mobilize our army? Did you think that this would be immediate?" Hannah stops for a second. He most certainly did think that all of this was happening immediately.

"It will be two weeks from now that we will have to worry about my battle with Pluie. More time and planning would be preferable, but Pluie can be impatient," Schwarz drowsily interjects. He shifts his legs, opens an eye, and decides not to roll over onto his side. No sense in squishing Ansel's sister. He seems to be rather attached to her. "No, for right now we can relax. We will have plenty to do in the next few days. I have to polish some armor, and you should brush up on your French. Pluie speaks modern French well enough, I suppose, but he will most likely speak ancient French to me. He thinks it makes him sound smart. He will do it to impress the French leaders,"

"I don't know French," Ansel's eyes go wide. He is so screwed if he is expected to know French. He knew Russian, Austrian, and Polish. French, not so much. He always thought it sounded too nasally to him, so he never bothered to learn it.

"You don't speak French? You live next to France! French was the common language not that long ago. You don't speak French," Schwarz sighs. Did things really change that much in a couple hundred years that French was no longer considered THE language to know? He doubts it. He is pretty sure it is just Ansel. There is just so much to teach the man.

"I know French. I'll help Ansel out," and with that Hannah invites herself along to this momentous, but hopefully fake, battle.

"Oh, no. You're going home where it is safe. I am not having you in battle. There is no way. Mom will never forgive me for leaving you two at the farm. She'd hunt me down and murder me, painfully, if I let you get hurt," Ansel objects. He loves his sister, he is not having her in the midst of a fight between two dragons.

"You know I'm older than you, right?" Hannah is singularly unimpressed with Ansel's protective outburst. She's been protecting her brother for YEARS against school bullies until he grew into his big, gangly feet and clumsy hands. She did not need his protection now. There was certainly no way she was missing a battle between two dragons.

"Yeah, well, I said no. You can't come." Ansel crosses his arms and leans back on his heels, bound and determined to appear as solid as the wall behind him.

"Well, I have to come," Hannah stops looking at her brother. She would burst into laughter if she keeps watching him try to look so tough.

"And why do you have to come?" Ansel knows he shouldn't ask. He knows he is just playing into her hand. She has him trapped with that small question. He knows it. He has spent his entire life learning her argument style. By now he should know not to further engage her, to walk away, but no, he has to ask.

"I have to go because you never learned French. If we're going against French soldiers, and a French dragon, then we will need to speak French at some time. Holding up your phone for Google Translate will not be effective. So, I will need to be there. Besides, someone will need to protect you and keep you from making any obvious blunders, like walking into a rain barrel or something." Hannah smiles to herself. Nothing like getting an appropriate dig against her brother to put the cherry on her Sunday.

"That only happened once!" Ansel turns red with embarrassment. Hannah will never let down the day that he walked into a rain barrel, and managed to fall into it! There was not even anything around it at the time. It was just a barrel, in a field, half full of water. He was not paying attention and managed to hit it just right that he folded right up and into it. He managed to pull himself out without injury or drowning, but not before Hannah saw it.

As for Google Translate, that was exactly what he was planning on using to communicate with any French soldiers that he might come across. If he was lucky, it would even be able to translate what Pluie had to say. Why wouldn't it work? It might be a little slower than having a translator, but it would be safer than having his "big" sister there.

"Why won't Google Translate work?" Ansel knows he is going to lose. *Might as well find out Hannah's reasoning so he had a better chance of winning next time. Yeah, I'll win next time. Sure...*

"Because of the accuracy issues with Google Translate. It does better if you can type in the words and have it translated that way, but you won't have that option. Instead, you will rely upon the voice recognition aspect of the app. If your microphone doesn't properly pick up their speech, you won't get a proper translation. Not to mention any accent that they might have, slurring, or lisping. There are a lot of factors in using Google Translate that most people don't actually acknowledge.

"Plus, if Pluie, which means Rain, by the way, is going to use ancient French, then there is a strong chance that Google Translate won't pick any of it up. Your only hope will be a human translator. Rather than hiring someone who does not know about dragons, you need me. I will translate for you, as needed," Hannah knows she won, so she sits smugly smiling against Schwarz, enjoying her victory.

"We could just get someone from the unicorns. They already know about dragons and the like, plus they will most likely know ancient French as well as modern French," Ansel might save his sister yet!

"No. We will not be going to the unicorns for this," Schwarz cuts in. "They, and we, cannot afford for them to become entangled in this mess. As it is, I, and Pluie, will both be seeing fines from the Unseen Treaty. The unicorns do not have the same amount of wealth that we dragons have. In addition, I will not risk one of their people for my issues. It would not be right. Instead, we will risk ourselves. Hannah comes, that's final."

Ansel thinks about arguing with Schwarz, but he knows when he is beaten. With a sigh, he drops down next to Hannah. "You know I worry about you, right?" He bumps his shoulder against hers, playfully.

"I know you do. You know I worry about you, too. Just as Mom would kill you if I get hurt, she'd murder me in my sleep if I let you walk into danger alone. Besides, you're not keeping me away from a dragon battle. I've been reading about them all my life. I will actually get to see one, live. This alone is worth the risk. And it is a risk we will take together," Hannah answers back, bumping his shoulder lightly.

"Of course, you want to see a dragon battle. And you're gonna wanna see the unicorns, and whatever else exists in this new world we find ourselves," Ansel sounds resigned to hauling his sister around the world to see all of the Magickals that she has spent her life reading about.

"I wonder if there are shapeshifters and werewolves and if they are anything at all like what they are in the books? Like, Patricia Briggs werewolves, and Ilona Andrews shapeshifters. That'd be totally worth leaving the rest of human society for," Hannah teases her little brother.

"Eww... I don't want to know! Leave the paranormal romances to the books, please," Ansel laughs in answer. Schwarz just watches them, amused and wondering as to who those authors were.

38

Chapter 38

The next couple of weeks are spent in an absolute rush. Yeah, they aren't going to war right away, but there is a lot that needs to be done. Bauer is almost a constant figure in the Palace in the Mount for the entire time. She becomes so prevalent of a fixture, that finding her taking a break and helping herself to a snack in the kitchen becomes commonplace. Her multitude of aides are far less informal and always made sure to bring their own food and to keep to the public domains of the palace.

For some reason, Bauer feels that she has developed a relationship with Schwarz, like an extended family almost. It could be that they both claim the people of Germany as theirs. It could be the loyalty that they tend to show those who are under their protection. They both had a tendency to micromanage everything when under pressure. All of this could be true. Or it could simply be that they were spending almost every waking moment trying to ensure the success of the joint military venture.

No matter the reasoning for the informality, it does not bother Schwarz in the least. He is very used to heads of state doing whatever they feel like, within reason. He has no concerns that Bauer would break the guesting laws, even if they are no longer considered a formal arrangement. Bauer never disappoints Schwarz either. She always brings a gift, usually food for Ansel and Hannah, and never takes anything that was not formally offered to her. It makes her very welcome in their home.

Throughout these meetings, Hannah and Ansel are kept busy with chores of their own. While they are never actually excluded from the meetings with Schwarz, it is very obvious that they are in over their heads and are frequently confused as to what is going on. Neither of the siblings has ever been in the military and are confused by the maneuvers and procedures that are discussed.

Many of the military leaders soon become frustrated, but did not show their frustration, frequently having to stop and explain everything repeatedly. To solve that, Schwarz gives them chores so they are not excluded from the preparations, but are not under the feet of the military leaders.

The chores consist primarily of polishing. All of their chores are polishing. They polish the straps to the harness that holds Ansel's traveling box. They polish the box. They polish armor. They polish swords. They polish lances. If it is metal, wood, or leather, it is polished. Just when they think they are done polishing, Schwarz would find another set of dragon armor to be polished.

"Don't we have people for all of this?" Ansel finally complains after the third set of armor is brought down to him by Schwarz. This set is elaborately decorated with enamel insets and gold filigree. Looking at it made his arms hurt. Hannah just looks at it as all hope of being done in the next century leaves her body.

"Yes, we could have other people clean the armor, the lances, the swords, and everything else. Then if it failed, we could say, 'But they were incompetent, and that's why I failed.' Because if the armor, sword, or lance fails, then you will fail. Armor and weapons are important pieces of equipment, and should only be cleaned and handled by those who are going to use them. Anything less is a cop-out, a way to sidestep the responsibility for the effectiveness of the tool," Schwarz does not scold Ansel for looking to take the easy way out, but he certainly does make it clear that he did expect Ansel to do the work.

"Then shouldn't it be you cleaning and polishing your armor?" Hannah asks. She does not mean it to sound accusing, but it sounds almost like an accusation. Here Schwarz was telling them that they could not pass the buck, but that's what he was doing, right?

"You're right, of course. I will be double-checking everything that you do with my armor and weapons. I am hoping that you decide you care enough to do the job properly, better than someone who is simply being paid for it. Rather, I would hope that you are doing it as someone who cares about the individual who will be wearing the armor and handling the weapons, namely, me. I will double-check it all, not out of a lack of trust in your intentions, but rather because you are so new to the process.

"You do not think that I am punishing you for not knowing or being in the way of the meetings, do you? It makes me happy that you two decided to try to help, rather than play games in your room or lounge in the library. By polishing and checking over the armor, weapons, and straps, you are making an active contribution in a way that best suits your skills and takes a concern off of my shoulders. I do hope that you know I appreciate your help." Schwarz looks at them each for a long moment.

They look tired. They have been getting up early every morning working on the pieces. They often went to bed after everyone else had left. Once he had even found them asleep at the table that they use to clean the smaller pieces. They need a break. He is just worried that they would be targets if they were to go into town and enjoy themselves for a day. This is a highly volatile time between Germany and France, even if they were hoping to avoid actual warfare and the average German citizen has no idea of what is going on.

"You two have been working very hard for a while now. Why don't I have Bauer assign some people to you and you guys go into town and enjoy yourselves. Get some coffee, see a movie, or whatever it is that you guys do to have fun. Get some shopping done. Buy something for your mother and have it sent to her. Do something that is not working here."

39

Chapter 39

Ansel makes the classic mistake of thinking that Hannah and he could just leave and enjoy a quiet afternoon together, not working. They no sooner attempt to leave and get in Ansel's car than they are stopped by Bauer's security. Schwarz had mentioned that he would get some of Bauer's people to be their security, but Ansel and Hannah do not actually think they need it. Nor did they think that they are important enough to Bauer for her to send her personal security with them. After all, they are just two kids, granted, they are actually in their twenties, and really just need a break.

Not only does Bauer send her security, but they insist on taking their armored cars. The security team also decides that two civilians driving was too much of a security risk, so they have to sit in the back like wayward children. It definitely sucks the fun right out of what could have been a fun little trip to Munich. The six soldiers that Bauer sends with them do not even give the siblings their names, Ansel and Hannah are supposed to just pretend that they aren't there.

"A lot easier to pretend that you're not here if I can drive and you sit in the back," Hannah tests. She is staring up at the soldier who appears to be the leader of the group. With her arms crossed in front of her, and a cocked hip, she does her best to look down at a guy who stood a foot and a half taller than she. Sometimes it actually worked. This is not one of those times.

The soldier she was attempting to stare down just looks at her, makes as though he would hand her the keys, and then snatches them back with a smirk before she could actually grab them. It takes all of her self-control not to kick the guy, but she guesses he would be ready for that and simply sidestep her or something. She would try flirting, he is handsome enough, but she is pretty sure that there was something against fraternizing with the person you were supposed to be protecting.

Resigning to being treated like children, they pile in the Rheinmetall Landsystemes, more commonly known as the Wolf, that the soldiers had driven up onto the mountain. This was not Bauer's vehicle, but rather the soldier's vehicle. It looks like a souped-up Jeep. It even carries the additional armor, making the vehicles small arms resistant.

Seating only four, two of the soldiers ride in front with Hannah and Ansel in the back, and the other four take a separate Wolf. This is not a sneaky ride into Munich, they would instead be sticking out like a sore thumb and attracting too much attention. There is not a lot of storage room for purchases, and it is not the most comfortable ride, but they are safe.

Hannah and Ansel are both rather surprised then when starting the vehicle, the radio turned on automatically, blasting AC/DC, loudly. With the silence of the six soldiers and their serious behaviors, they firmly expected a silent ride. Instead, no sooner than the radio turns on so do the personalities of those soldiers.

"I'm Fischer," the soldier in the front passenger seat says, turning around to face the siblings. "That's Wagner," Fischer says as he points to the driver. Wagner taps his head with his forefinger at the sound of his name. "Where are we off to?"

Ansel looks over at his sister hoping she has a good idea. She knows their mother the best. "I think I want to go to Roly Poly. Schwarz had a good idea when he suggested sending a gift to our Mom. I think some good quilting material might make it so we eventually can walk into our home without her killing us on sight, or at least making us wish she'd have killed us," Hannah answers with a smile. Ansel knows that smile might be to disarm the soldier and make him think she is joking about their mother. She is not though.

"Roly Poly?" Wagner makes the name a question. "Where is that?"

"It's on Fraunhoferstraße. Don't worry, I won't let us get lost," Hannah answers, leaning forward so that she can talk over the music and right to Wagner. She does not want him to miss a turn and get frustrated. She has no intention of returning to the Palace in the Mount early because they got lost.

***

Pulling away from the Mountain, they never notice the small flash of a pair of binoculars hiding on a back road in the woods. They are well on their way before the holder of those binoculars slowly makes his way down the mountain with his companion, trailing after the pair of vehicles.

***

True to her word, Hannah is able to guide Wagner to Roly Poly without mishap. The second Wolf, with the other four soldiers, follows tightly to their tail the entire time, so they also have no problem getting to Roly Poly, even though they have no idea where they are heading. Ansel could only imagine their surprise when they pulled up to a quilt shop, of all places.

Hannah initially hops right out of the Wolf, expecting to waltz into the store. She is immediately stopped by Wagner. His smile is gone, and he stands like a wall, blocking her path. How one person became a wall is something Hannah couldn't quite understand, but he does it. He is as effective at blocking her as a brick wall down the middle of a street. Ansel, who had followed a little more slowly, hesitates in the car.

The cause of this sudden blocking becomes obvious as the other four soldiers take up surrounding positions. Once the road is deemed as safe as it is going to get and they determine which store they are going into, two of the men walk into the store to check it. The only patron in the store is hastily escorted out, and only then can Hannah and Ansel go in.

The inside of Roly Poly is a fabric heaven. There are quilt and sewing kits lining the walls. There are bolts of material throughout the room, handmade clothes, purses, and totes hang on pegs and hooks. This small store, more a hole in the wall than anything else, is like a magical portal to another world where everything was soft, comfortable, and warm. Ansel could easily see his mother loving the place.

Hannah wastes no time at all picking out some beautiful materials and a quilt pattern. Ansel catches her checking prices as she is going through, and calmly informs her that they could afford it, and not to worry about it. To simply get what she feels their mother will like and something for herself as well.

Finally, after an hour of wandering around, touching almost all of the fabric, and picking out a pile's worth of goods, Hannah is satisfied with her purchases. She now has enough quilting material to make three large quilts, and she even got herself a nice peasant-style shirt and a beautiful purse. The store's motto, Take it or Make it, is very much in evidence on this visit. Everything but Hannah's purchases are sent to their mother's home, directly from the store.

"Now where, sister?" Ansel asks.

"Coffee? And then sushi?"

"Sounds great!" Ansel answers with enthusiasm. He really likes sushi, and Devi, their chef, absolutely hated making sushi. He hates it so much that he had yet to consent to making sushi, and even though Ansel knows that he is paying the man to make food, and therefore sushi should be on the menu. He is not desperate enough to piss off the man who made 90% of his meals. Instead, every time he really wants sushi, he leaves to get it, and today looks like a sushi day.

40

Chapter 40

Alas, there is to be no sushi. Instead, the men who had watched their departure from the mountain, the same ones that no one had managed to spot, decide at that moment to attack. Hannah and Ansel are finally given the all-clear to step out the door of the shop and onto a busy street. Four of the soldiers had blocked off the sidewalk leading to their car, but there are still people everywhere.

Without extensive planning as to a route that they were going to travel and a little more than a moment's warning, the guards are unable to block off the entire street. This makes doing threat assessments harder than it normally would be. Years of practice and experience are the only things giving the guards the confidence that they need to do the job well. That and a lot of practice with the worst-case scenarios.

Hannah and Ansel are not on their guard. They are not paying attention to the crowd. They feel safe in the streets of Munich. They feel it is overkill to have guards with them at all. They are certain that everyone is overreacting and that nothing wrong could ever happen to them, despite the insanity that their lives are currently experiencing. They are not heads of state, dragons, or even people of importance. The idea that they might be a target for anyone but another dragon, which they are fairly certain they would see coming, never even crosses their minds. That is why they stop and stand like deer in headlights when the gunshots go off.

Luckily for Ansel and Hannah, Fischer is not so slow on the mark. He bodily grabs them and throws them into the car where they might be safer before launching himself over the front of the Wolf and into the passenger seat. Wagner had not gotten out of the car when they went into Roly Poly but rather stayed in the car to ensure a quick exit if necessary, and it does appear that a quick exit is necessary. He pulls out quickly and takes off down the street with Fischer barely in the passenger seat.

The sound of gunfire chases them down the narrow street as the remaining four men take on an enemy that neither Hannah nor Ansel has yet to see. The fact that they are the targets of an attack hardly seemed possible to them. Who would want to kill two people with no real power or money? They sorely underestimate their value to Schwarz and therefore to Bauer. They have no idea that they might be the two most valuable people in Germany at that moment.

"Are you two okay?" Fischer asks once they clear the road. One glance tells him that they are frightened, but he doesn't see or smell any blood, so he doesn't think that they have been injured. Next time he would make sure that they are armored, so if someone shot at them, and hit them, it wouldn't kill them. They are lucky, and he hates to rely on luck.

Hannah looks at him for a moment, shocky and confused. She glances over at her brother who is huddled next to her. Time to be the oldest that she is. She takes a deep breath, closes her eyes for a second, and counts to five silently. When she opens them again, she gives Fischer a smile that does not quite touch her eyes, "Yeah, I think we're alright. Or at least we will be alright. Thank you."

Grasping Ansel's arm she draws his attention to her. "You are alright. You're scared, but you are not hurt." Hannah does not ask, she tells Ansel that he is alright.

She used to do that way back when they were young and he would do something that scared him, like falling out of a tree. Granted, this was a little bit more dangerous and scary than a tree, but she knew that it would work to calm him down. After all, no matter how old they are, she is still his older sister. He would still listen to her.

Ansel for his part looks up at his sister. He knows she is right, that neither one of them are hurt. She just reaffirms it and he finds it reassuring. He then notices Fischer watching them, assessing them. He smiles at both Hannah and Fischer, then sits up in his seat. "I guess we're not going for coffee and sushi, then."

"No, unfortunately not. Instead, we're gonna meet up with the other Wolf and return home," Wagner answers from the driver's seat. "I was really looking forward to getting a cup of coffee, and sushi sounds really good right about now. We can thank whoever it was that shot at us for the ruined plans and empty bellies." Wagner sounds rather upset about the whole thing. Hannah reaches up and puts a hand on his shoulder in consolation.

41

Chapter 41

After a few minutes of driving through random streets, in absolute silence, the radio barks some static and a breathless man's voice. It makes Hannah and Ansel jump. "All clear. One of them is dead, but we got the other one, and their vehicle. We'll meet you up at the meeting point Alpha." It is one of the soldiers that went with Hannah and Ansel, but whose name they do not know yet.

"Rodger that," Fischer answers back. He then changes the channel on the overly complicated-looking radio and calls his boss at the Mount. "Mount base, contact at Roly Poly, hatchlings secure and en route to rendezvous point A."

"Mount base, ambush site clear, one KIA one WIA, need Medevac at Roly Poly. Casualty is Litter Urgent, GSW to the right midsection and left arm. Buddy aid was applied, no medic on site. No friendly casualties, over," is immediately heard from the same channel. It is the other Wolf reporting in. No one on their side had been injured, but it sounds like the attacker is pretty injured. Hannah and Ansel are both a bit more surprised that the attacker was alive at all.

Rendezvous Point A is a decent-sized warehouse that has been cleared out and modified to provide a safe spot if necessary. The Wolf drives through garage doors that open automatically upon receiving the RFF signal from the vehicle. It is almost immediately joined by two additional Wolf vehicles and eight additional soldiers. Once everything is secure, Fischer gets his first good look at the siblings.

It is exactly as he thought, he had bruised both Hannah and Ansel when he tossed them in the back. Hannah had a small bump on her forehead where she ended up hitting the car door, from the inside, but she could not actually remember doing that, and it did not hurt her until Fischer points it out. Ansel only has a bruise on his arm from when Fischer grabbed him, but he looks more shaken up than Hannah.

One of the soldiers that had arrived as their backup while they waited for the other Wolf vehicle, happened to be a medic. Ansel is certain this was intentional, but he does not comment on it. She is the one who applies the cold patch to Hannah's head and to both of their arms. "Thank you for getting us out of there, Wagner and Fischer. We both froze up like idiots back there," Ansel says, watching the medic check Hannah for any sign of a concussion.

"No problem. I would not worry too much about freezing up. It happens to a lot of people, especially if they did not actually think they could ever be a target for any hostilities. I'm just glad you two did not fight me when I threw you in the car. You would be surprised how many times I've heard from bodyguards about the people who they are supposed to be protecting actually getting mad at them for doing their job." Fischer's body is relaxed, his face calm. It has a very calming effect on everyone around him. He is a natural leader. He even has a small smile playing on his lips, letting everyone know that everyone and everything is okay.

A few minutes later, and the other Wolf vehicle that had gone to Roly Poly with them arrives. It is shy of two men, but that is because those men were assigned to accompany their attacker to the hospital, via the ambulance. He is not going to get away, disappear, or otherwise not answer for his actions. Those men would be met at the hospital with their own backup.

Once everyone is assembled in the warehouse, it is time to return to the Palace in the Mount. This time Hannah and Ansel do not get to ride together in a single Wolf. This time they are separated into two different vehicles, with another vehicle leading them. They also are not wildly comfortable during the drive this time. The Wolf is designed to sit 4, and yet, they sat 5 a piece.

Hannah and Ansel each find themselves squished between two men on either side of them, making them the protected center of the car. Neither of them like the idea of others risking their lives for them, but they have to admit, it is better than dying.

Schwarz meets them as they are on their way up the road to the primary garage door. He looks at each of the three vehicles closely, then watches down the road as though he is expecting another attack. Not a single bird chirped or insect buzzed for fear of attracting his wrath, so angry was the dragon of Germany that his people were attacked.

Even though he was told that Ansel and Hannah were both safe and relatively unharmed, he would not calm down until he had checked them over himself. For being so big, he is incredibly gentle with Hannah as he examines the bump on her head. Fischer was concerned that he would be a goner for injuring her as he got her out of danger, but Schwarz just thanks him and moved on to Ansel. Schwarz knows the difficulties that can be experienced when moving a person from a battle scene.

"I am glad you two were not further injured in this attack. I understand that we have one of the two attackers in custody and that he is expected to make a full recovery from his gunshot wounds. We will find out who attacked you and why. They will wish that they had never heard of your name. And if this was Pluie's doing, well, he may have sealed his own fate." Schwarz is quiet as he talks to Hannah and Ansel. That does not mean that his words did not fall like hammers of truth when he spoke of retribution.

Everyone quickly enters the Palace in the Mount, seeking the security of an entire mountain above them. It amazed Ansel how quickly this place had become his home, that now he would seek shelter there. As they walk through the Palace, leaving Ansel and Hannah at the small, private kitchen, Schwarz turns to Bauer. "I will go with you, or your representative, to interrogate the prisoner. I wish to hear from his own lips who hired him and what he possibly felt could be gained by going after my people."

Bauer just looks up at Schwarz for a moment, picturing this giant dragon attempting to enter the hospital. There was a chance that he could enter the emergency bay doors. There was even a chance that he could fit in the lobby.

There is no chance he could even crawl through the narrow hallways, go up the stairs, or enter an elevator to get to the man in custody. The image itself is almost comical. "That might pose a few difficulties. He is being held in a secure wing of the hospital or rather will be after his surgery. The halls are quite narrow and the only access point is hampered by elevators and stairs. We might be able to bring him outside, to you, if he is in stable enough condition."

"Oh, I would not worry about that so much. I have ways to handle human-sized buildings. Just guarantee me that I will be allowed to question the individual." Schwarz does not look at Bauer as they speak, walking back to the office that they tended to favor for the strategy discussions that they have been conducting.

"If you can make it into a human-sized building, then yes, you are more than welcome to question the prisoner, in a humane manner. I cannot allow you to injure or torture the person in any way. It goes against the Geneva Convention and human decency." Bauer might have a hard time picturing Schwarz in a hospital, but she has no problem picturing him eating a man, piece by piece.

"I'll be on my best behavior." Schwarz smiles in a very non-convincing way. Bauer hesitates for a moment and then continues walking alongside the dragon.

"The man should be out of surgery later today. I plan on visiting him tomorrow, late morning. Would you like us to meet with you before that?" Bauer is hoping to get some clue as to how Schwarz is planning on being able to fit in the hospital.

"Yes, I will need you to come here before you go there. I will need a ride," and with that, Schwarz just smiles and walks away.

42

Chapter 42

The next morning, at ten, Bauer and her caravan of people arrive. An additional car, specifically for Schwarz, had been included in the caravan. It looks like an odd, large snake coming up the hill. Ansel greets them at the door, looking no worse for wear after yesterday's ordeal. If anything, he appears to have a bit of an impish smile on his face.

"Hello. We are here at the request of Schwarz. He said that he would need a ride to visit one of the men who attacked you. I assume that ride is for you?" Bauer greets Ansel, standing directly in front of him. She does not attempt to shake his hand or greet him informally. Normally they dispense with greetings all together, but today felt different.

"No, that's not for me. I was told to stay in the Palace from the moment Schwarz leaves until he comes back. That needed ride is for Schwarz since he does not know how to drive my car yet, although I suspect he will want to learn shortly after experiencing your car," Ansel answers. Again, he has that small smirk. He definitely knows something that they do not know, and he is eager for them to learn.

"Did I ever tell you how I met Schwarz?" Ansel asks in a seemingly non sequitur.

"No, I do not think we have ever discussed that," Bauer responds. It seemed like a weird thing to discuss while they wait for Schwarz to make himself known.

"Well, I might be a country bumpkin, but I know not to approach dragons. Instead, I got taken in by a beautiful woman, who I later happened to find out was a dragon. Matter of fact, here she is, now." Ansel smiles wide as he looks back, behind him.

Schwarz quickly approached the cars, walking with all the confidence of the biggest, baddest monster around. The effect is slightly spoiled by the fact that Schwarz, at that moment, looks like a small, young woman with silver-blond hair and piercing blue eyes. Her skin is creamy, and nearly as pale as milk. She is dressed in a formal gown if a simple one. It is a deep green satin with a square neckline and trailing hem. A gold belt worked with green dragons was wrapped around her waist.

"Bauer, I assume we are ready to go?" Schwarz looks up into Bauer's eyes, steady and demanding.

"Schwarz?" Bauer could not have been more surprised if Ansel had dropped and turned into a puppy right before her. She had many thoughts as to how Schwarz could possibly fit in a hospital. Quite a few of them ended with Schwarz dismantling the building. In no dream of hers, her husband's, or her children's, did she think that Schwarz, the giant-sized, and male, dragon would turn into a slip of a woman.

"The one and the same. Let's go," Schwarz answers. He, now she, walks to the cars and waits next to the first one in the line. She glares at one of the soldiers, waiting for him to open the door for her. After all, now she was in her human form, she expects to be treated like the human royalty she would be equivalent to, although she does far outrank any royalty she had ever heard of.

Bauer looks over to Ansel with questions in her eyes. He just smiles, nods, and waves as he goes back into the palace and shuts the door. They could have fun dealing with Schwarz, as a lady. He is certainly not less demanding in female, or human, form than he is as a male dragon. Nor does Ansel think he requires any more assistance or that he is any less dangerous as a woman. It would do well for everyone to remember that Schwarz may look helpless, but he most certainly is not.

***

The ride to the hospital where the prisoner is being kept under guard is unusually quiet. No one really knows what to say to a dragon, who is now a human. Especially with the added complication that a gender shift entailed. "Well, Schwarz, what made you take this form?" Bauer finally asks. It is killing her not knowing.

"Hum? Oh, this body? I have always preferred the female shape when I have to be human-sized. Before Ansel, all of my pets had been female, so it kept everything simple. I could have wove a male form, but I am very used to this one. Does it bother you?" Schwarz's voice is melodic and smooth. It is not quite soft, but very far from harsh. It is a cultured, practiced voice.

"No. You taking a human woman's form does not bother me. It was just rather surprising. Will you need any extra protections in this form?"

Schwarz gives a light chuckle at the idea of these people feeling the need to protect him. "No. I retain all my strength, all my defenses, and all my cunning, no matter what form I take."

"There are other forms?"

"I can be anything that I need to be. Obviously, being in my natural form, that of a dragon, is most preferable. But I can be anything from a dog to an elf if need be. I am always me in any of those forms, although not all of them have the advantages of speech or articulated hands. I tend to avoid the more useless forms," Schwarz answers. He had not meant to tell her as much about his shapeshifting abilities as he did, but what is done is done. It is not a skill he uses often and if they are going to interact as much as they have, there is a solid chance Bauer would have found out anyway.

"What can you tell me about the man that we are about to see?" Schwarz changes the topic suddenly. He wants answers for what happened yesterday. He feels as though a direct attack on his person has occurred, and he is not about to tolerate that.

Bauer looks at Schwarz for a second, shifting her mindset. "His name is Matteo Moulin. He has been gainfully employed in La Flotte, France as a shopkeeper for the past ten years. He has no known affiliates here in Germany.

What he is doing here is not certain. We speculate that he is here to do something related to the invasion that Pluie is planning, although we are uncertain what that something is."

"La Flotte? Pluie still runs that little town of his? Every person in that town is a member of his household, the last I knew. I rather doubt that has changed. If he's from La Flotte, he is most likely here to ensure that I come to the battle. Pluie would not hesitate to use innocent bait to get me to fight. The right bastard that he is.

"The question then becomes, did Pluie send this man to attack my people, to spy, or did this man act on his own to curry favor. To act so directly against another dragon is very much unlike Pluie's style, although he might be looking for some type of advantage. This might have even been the excuse that Pluie needs to make attacking Germany look righteous, rather than an insane plan to rebuild an obsolete empire." Schwarz sits back in his seat, brushing his long, silver hair out of his eyes. He spends the rest of the ride in silence, watching the world go by in the fastest and smoothest chariot he has ever ridden in.

43

Chapter 43

G roßhadern Clinic, the university hospital in Munich looks very much like a white brick with small holes in it, from a distance. It is the very definition of a rectangle. The utilitarian appearance ends at the exterior though. Inside, the hospital takes on a much more appealing air, with brightly colored corridors and spacious hallways. It was a far cry from the last hospital that Schwarz had visited, where you were far more likely to die going in than staying out of the hospital to heal.

The entourage escorting Bauer and Schwarz drives up the wide pathway leading directly to the entrance of the hospital's lobby. This is normally used as a footpath, but the security risk of Bauer and Schwarz both walking along what is normally a busy path put the soldiers on more edge than they already are. It is not worth the risk. So, instead, students and visitors are inconvenienced for a moment while the party drives up.

From there, they enter the lobby and are immediately met by security, the doctor in charge of the hospital, and Moulin's doctor. The security personnel look like former wrestlers who continue to get their exercise by dealing with unruly patients. They are quickly dismissed by the soldiers who escort Bauer and Schwarz though.

The Head Doctor looks more like a pencil pusher than anything else. He wears a button-up shirt and ties under his white coat. His pants look freshly pressed. He does not look like he has handled patients in a very long time.

Schwarz immediately dismisses him from his mind. This was not the man who would be able to give him good answers about the man he is here to see.

The other doctor looks like he just got done working with the man in question. He is well dressed but in a more worn way. His clothes are clean under his white coat, but they are not freshly pressed. If anything, they look like he quickly brushed them down and then ran down flights of stairs to meet up with them. Schwarz immediately likes him. He introduces himself to the party as Doctor Braum.

They talk as they walk. The terms are all very technical, and Schwarz quickly finds himself tuning them out. Once the doctors wound themselves down, he asks for a recap, in layman's terms, please.

"Moulin's prognosis is quite good, despite the severity of his injuries. Normally we would not allow non-family visitors this early on, but an exception has been made. He is on very strong medication though, so his answers should be considered suspect and any outbursts forgiven," Doctor Braum answers, looking directly at Schwarz. It appears he has identified the highest threat to his patient well enough.

It is not long after that statement that they are outside of the prisoner's door. Two police officers are standing outside the door. There are two more inside the room, watching the patient. There is no television or radio playing. The room is all but silent, with the only noise being the beeping of the machinery monitoring the man's vital signs.

The steady beeping that had been the only sound in the room abruptly increases their paces when Moulin sees who walks into his room. The dragon might be in disguise, but he knows his death when he sees it. There is no mistaking the woman for anything but what she really is, a dragon, not to someone who knows dragons like he does.

Matteo Moulin is a scared, young man. His blue eyes have white showing all the way around the irises. His skin is pale and shines with sweat. He trembles sporadically in his bed, rattling the cuffs that secure him in place. He does not want to face the people who walked into the room, but rather steals glances at them from the corners of his eyes, almost as though he is afraid that looking at them directly would make the situation worse.

Doctor Braum is the first to approach Moulin. His rapid and confident steps quickly take him to the man's side, where he places a hand on the Moulin's shoulder in comfort. He quickly glances at the various readings on the monitors and then speaks quietly to Moulin. "These people are here to talk to you about yesterday. They will not hurt you. It is in your best interests to be honest with them. But before that, I need you to calm down. Why don't we practice breathing together."

Schwarz watches the men as Braum leads Moulin in breathing exercises. His estimation of this doctor went up several more notches. Not everyone knows that the fastest way to get answers is to slow down, but this man does. As they breathe together, Schwarz notices the heavy bandages and drainage tubes coming from the man's abdomen. In his time, such a wound would not have been survivable. Secretly, Schwarz is even more impressed. Once the man's breathing and heart rates fall into a more steady rhythm, Bauer is able to begin.

Bauer starts by taking a seat next to the man's bedside so that they are at the same level, rather than her standing over him. Schwarz, now intrigued with this new style of interrogation, takes a seat next to Bauer. He marvels even more when Bauer turns from being the leader of Germany to being someone's grandmother. Bauer becomes approachable.

"Do you know who I am?" Bauer asks. Her tone is soft, respectful, and pleasant. She sounds like someone you want to please, not just someone you are expected to respect. She also addresses him in French, which also catches Schwarz off guard. He knows French, and he should not have been surprised that Bauer did, but he is more than surprised that she addresses this man in his native language. In the old days, his interrogators would have made their demands in German, despite the prisoner speaking only French. It was not an efficient time.

"You're Mrs. Bauer. You are the Chancellor of Germany. I am in so much trouble, aren't I," Moulin answers, also in French. His voice is small and scared. He sounds even younger than he really is.

"Do you know who is sitting next to me?" Bauer does not answer his question. It is not time yet. She wants to get everyone named first. She knows that they are recording this interview, even if Moulin does not know that yet.

Moulin looks over at Schwarz and immediately down to his bed. "That is Schwarz, the Sky's Darkness, King Dragon of Germany," he all but whispers. Schwarz hasn't heard those titles in hundreds of years, since well before his curse, but he remembers burning them into the minds of everyone. Apparently, Pluie and his lot have not forgotten.

"And who are you?" Bauer continues. Bauer does not even question the titles. Of course, a dragon would have titles, and of course, those titles would make no sense.

"I'm Matteo Moulin. I am the owner of Jingles, a small shop in La Flotte, France."

"How did you know that this..." man, woman, dragon, "... person... next to me is Schwarz?" Pronouns and nouns are complicated when someone can change shape at will.

"They have been circulating images and pictures of the heavy players in the upcoming battle between Pluie's army and Germany. Your picture, the boy, Ansel's picture, and images of what Schwarz might look like at any given time. My brother, Marcel, and I went after Ansel yesterday, it would have been surprising if Schwarz did not make an appearance.

"I have never met Pluie before he began gathering his army, and I've only seen him from a distance since then, but I have heard all about how his kind is protective of what they decide is theirs. I knew Ansel was Schwarz's. I tried to take him anyway. I expect punishment for that action." Moulin does not face Bauer but rather keeps his head down towards his pillows. He looks very much like a man who has given up on life, expecting it to be taken away from him at any moment.

"I'm unlikely to kill or punish you if you cooperate with Bauer's questions," Schwarz reassures. He is not surprised that the man does not claim to know Pluie well. Pluie was always a little bit standoffish with his people, keeping a small number close to him while claiming entire towns. Moulin looks up at him with surprise, and Schwarz gives him a closed-lip smile in support.

This new, gentle interrogation method is so at odds with the old methods that Schwarz was used to. They spend a lot of their time getting to know the man, setting him at ease, and making sure he is comfortable. Only after they are certain that they understand the man for who he is, do they attempt to understand what happened yesterday.

"To be honest, the whole thing was a spur-of-the-moment decision. My brother and I were only supposed to watch the Palace from a distance, to make sure Schwarz was going to appear on the battlefield. We were supposed to call in as soon as we saw Schwarz leave, heading for France. We were also to report anyone coming or going from the Palace. We did this via cell phone since radio transmissions were more likely to be intercepted."

"But you're a store owner. Surely Pluie had people who were better trained for that type of surveillance," Schwarz interjects. He might have sent Ansel to meet with Bauer in the first place, but that's because Ansel was the only person he had. Pluie has hundreds of people, possibly even thousands.

"We're a tourist town. We don't have a standing military. We barely have a police station. It would have been a French soldier, except Pluie really wanted it to be his people who watched over the Palace, so I was told to do it. I brought my brother along to help me. I thought we'd get honors, instead, I got my brother killed," Moulin sobs that last part. Everyone is silent as he gets himself back under control, with Doctor Braum watching the monitors like a hawk to ensure that he is in no danger of setting back his recovery.

"What made you change your plans and go after Ansel? He was pretty well guarded and it was just you two," Bauer asks in a soft voice once the man has himself under control.

"It was impulsive and stupid. You see, there was a lot of concern that Schwarz would not come out of his Palace to fight for the Germans. This did not bother the French soldiers, but it bothered Pluie. He wanted to defeat Schwarz in front of Papillon and show off for his lady. When we reported that Ansel left with a group of people, we were told to stay put. Marcel had this idea that we'd go and kidnap Ansel, presenting him to Pluie as a trophy. That would ensure that Schwarz came onto the battlefield. We figured the girl was his friend and therefore kidnapping her was also a good idea. It did not go anywhere near as planned. We did not stand a chance of getting near them, but we tried anyway.

"We followed them to a quilting store, of all places. We watched as they cleared the store and people from the sidewalks to let Ansel and the girl in. We waited just past the cars for them to come out. The plan was to grab them, and then run back to our car, leaving immediately before anyone could react. Marcel thought that he could use gunfire to distract the soldiers, and increase our chances of getting away with Ansel. He was our target.

"No sooner than the soldiers began filing out of the store with Ansel and we started approaching, did they react. They were fast. They saw us as a threat. They did not see the gunshots as a threat, just an annoyance. They took us down fast, too fast. Marcel did not stand a chance. I got hit in the arm and stomach, but he got hit in the head.

"My last sight of my brother will always be the look of surprise on his face as he went down," Moulin is a very cooperative prisoner. Being nice and building a sense of rapport with the prisoner works very well. Schwarz will have to remember this technique in the future. It does not hurt that this is no professional spy and he does not know any secrets to keep. Either way, Schwarz is very confident with the information the man is giving. It fits very well with the evidence that they had found in his vehicle, which included a notebook with the comings and goings of the Palace in the Mount.

"Is there anyone you would like us to contact?" and at Bauer's question, the man goes from a comfortable state to one of terror once again.

"Don't call Pluie!! Please don't call Pluie! He'll have me executed. He might even have me drawn and quartered!" Matteo begins trying to scramble out of bed and away from Bauer and Schwarz. Everyone reacts fast. Schwarz and Bauer grab the man, holding him onto the bed, Schwarz by his legs, and Bauer by his arms. Doctor Braum launches himself off the wall and to the man's head. The soldiers in the room tense to tackle him if he should get off the bed. He does not have a snowball's chance in hell of escape, but he tries. It is tense for several seconds until he is subdued. Apparently, everyone forgot that he is cuffed, and could not have gotten away if he had tried.

"We won't call Pluie if that's what you want. But surely there is someone who cares about you and wants to know if you are safe. If not, we will not risk your life by informing your dragon master that you are here and managed to do something very stupid. We do need to inform the Prime Minister of France though. She needs to know where you are, but we will not release you into anyone's custody for the time being. You will be our guest." With that, Bauer and Schwarz stand and leave. They have to call the Prime Minister of France.

Chapter 44

Bauer and Schwarz leave the hospital the same way that they came in. As they walk down the cleared halls, Bauer offers to allow Schwarz to accompany her to her office to call Camille Dupont, the Prime Minister of France. Bauer does not expect Schwarz to agree, after all, Schwarz has his own comfortable office in which they could call Dupont, but instead, Schwarz agrees enthusiastically. "I am very interested in what your offices are like. You have seen my place, it is only fitting that I get to see yours as well."

Where the hospital is very utilitarian to the max, Bauer's office building is an art sculpture that comes to life. The entire building is a series of curves in white stone. Even the white security gates have the flair of artistry to them. The inside of the building matches the outside, with wide corridors, and ample light. They skip the security stations, not wishing to subject Schwarz to the modern systems and risk insulting the dragon on his very first visit to the seats of power in Germany.

Instead, they take a direct route to Bauer's office, stopping only to request refreshments of an aid. In short order, Schwarz finds himself in a wide, airy white room with blonde wood furniture. It feels more like someone's living room than an office. There is a wall of books and plaques, a round meeting table, and her desk. Schwarz is instantly comfortable. The cakes, coffee, tea, and water that are brought up as refreshments are a most welcome addition to the homey feel of the room.

Once Schwarz is comfortable, Bauer places a call to France. It does not take long to get a hold of Camille Dupont. Bauer and her have become quite close and communicated frequently over the past few weeks, trying to ensure that the peace in the nations is maintained and that World War III does not result from the meddlings of a dragon. That is not to say that she is expecting Bauer's call. Not at all, instead it interrupts another phone call with another nation, but the wait is not particularly long.

It also does not take long for Bauer to explain exactly what happened and that now they have a French prisoner from the French dragon. "Moulin has no intention of being returned to France or to Pluie. He feels that he will be executed if he returns to the dragon. We can continue to house him here, but if you want him back, we will cooperate with you," Bauer finishes in French.

Camille Dupont sits so still that Bauer thought that she had lost the transmission feed for a moment. It is a serious issue, to be sure, but no one was hurt so no repercussions need to be taken. Schwarz even seems to be ready to forgive, if not to forget. Granted, Dupont had been dealing almost exclusively with Pluie, so she is most likely caught off guard by the offer to return the prisoner or to house him without further demands.

"That is very interesting. I will get back to you on that. I will have to talk with Pluie's representatives. They were here yesterday asking for assistance in finding a couple rouge agents. I have to assume that these are the individuals they are looking for. I, personally, have no objections to Moulin staying in Germany, under your supervision. I think he might be safer there.

"Schwarz, I apologize for the actions of one of the citizens of my country. They never should have made a move against you or your people. I do hope that Ansel and his sister are alright. Please offer them my humblest apologies," Dupont finally says.

"It is quite alright. People will always act rashly and you can hardly fault your country for the actions of a couple of men who have been trained since birth to view a dragon as the ruler, not you. I hold Pluie in more fault than you, or your country. You are safe from retribution from me." If Dupont is surprised to find Schwarz is now a human woman, she does not show it. After all, why not, why couldn't the world's fiercest predator also change shape.

"As for Ansel and Hannah. They are fine. They are more upset that they could not get their coffee and sushi than that they were almost kidnapped. They were not hurt, just a little scared. They are resilient, they will be okay." Schwarz does his best to reassure Dupont that he did not hold her or her country at fault. After all, Dupont was helping them all avoid war. She could have simply done as Pluie demanded and attacked Germany, keeping her country safe from the dragon but damning both nations to war.

"I am glad to hear that. I will call shortly with details regarding the decision on Moulin. Incidentally, the next meeting is with Pluie's war counsel," and with that, Dupont clicks off the monitor.

Schwarz and Bauer sit there for a moment. "She did not seem surprised that you were here in the form of a woman," Bauer eventually comments.

"She has most likely met Papillon. Papillon is not opposed to taking a human shape, if necessary. Granted, Papillon is female all of the time, no matter what the form. Papillon looks a lot like a red-blond version of me in human form. We are siblings, after all," Schwarz answers. He is busy thinking about what he would do if he had to return Moulin. Not that there is anything he could do.

"You are related to one of the dragons who is trying to invade?" Bauer turns and looks at Schwarz sharply. This is information that she would have liked to have had weeks ago. But no, she is just learning it now.

For his part, Schwarz did not even think about mentioning Papillon was his sister before, it seemed irrelevant. "Well, yes. Papillon is my sister. Pluie and I are not related. Papillon is most likely simply going with whatever Pluie wants. She has never been interested in human politics and couldn't care less about the Holy Roman anything. I did not think it was worth mentioning, she won't come onto the battlefield."

"Any other surprises I should be aware of?" Bauer asks Schwarz.

"It wouldn't be a surprise if you were told about it, now would it. I have no idea what you think is relevant, and I have no idea where to start with telling you about the histories between our peoples or my personal history. If we run across anything else, I will let you know as I think of it," Schwarz closes his eyes as he speaks. He is getting tired. It has been a long day, and maintaining a human shape is taxing. "If you would be so kind as to call a car, I would like to return home."

45

Chapter 45

The car ride back to the Palace in the Mount is quiet. While Bauer offered guards, all Schwarz really needs is a driver. He is absolutely certain that if someone were stupid enough to attack the car, he would be the one doing the guarding and saving, not the other way around. Bauer could not argue against that. Instead, it is a single driver and Schwarz in a small sedan. Schwarz rides in the front, enjoying the experience and playing with the radio quietly.

As soon as the car turns around and disappears down the drive, Schwarz strips from the dress that he was wearing. It is a comfortable dress, but he is far more accustomed to being naked and the feel of the material on human skin is irritating. Ansel is far less accustomed to opening doors to greet Schwarz and finding a naked woman standing there though. He throws up his hands, shielding his eyes from the figure standing there. "Clothes or scales!" Ansel yells.

"What is wrong with you?" Schwarz asks tiredly, as he shifts into his normal giant green dragon shape.

"Women do not typically walk around naked. If they happen to be undressed, it is polite not to look," Ansel answers, finally dropping his hand from his eyes once Schwarz finishes his transformation.

"You don't find my human form attractive?" Schwarz teases gently.

"Oh, the form is pretty enough. But, I know it is you in there, and last I checked, you were a male dragon. I'm not into that," Ansel answers back, scooping up the discarded dress. He would leave it for the laundry crew to figure out how to wash and preserve it. It has lasted a couple hundred years, there is no reason it could not last a couple more hundred years.

"You are so repressed. Not that I'm complaining. It saves me having to get you fixed." Schwarz laughs as he finishes talking. It never gets old teasing Ansel about getting him fixed and that look of horror Ansel gets every time.

Ansel, however, feels that the joke is very old. He is tired of hearing about it and simply rolls his eyes. "Yeah, yeah, repressed, fixed... sure." Changing the subject seems like a good idea, "How did it go with that guy, the prisoner? Any juicy facts or conspiracies?"

"No, no juicy facts or conspiracies. Just a man who made a stupid choice. Bauer talked with him. He was sent here to watch our comings and goings, and he and his brother thought they saw an opportunity to impress Pluie. They failed, one died, and the other is being held at the hospital. He was actually quite talkative. I think he was expecting torture."

"Bauer talked to him? She speaks French or he speaks German?" Ansel is surprised at either option.

"Bauer speaks French. I was not surprised to find that the man, Moulin, does not speak German."

"I'm surprised that Bauer speaks French. Her public biography does not mention it."

"You looked her up? You do know that people are allowed to have secrets, right?" Schwarz is a little surprised that Ansel would bother looking up Elisabeth Bauer. He dealt with the woman almost every day, so why bother looking up stuff when you could just ask her? But how was he to understand this modern age? It has been two hundred years since he dealt with people and the world in general.

"Uh, yeah, well, you know. Or maybe you don't. I like to know who I'm dealing with on a daily basis. I looked into the public profiles of everyone we deal with every day. I don't seem to find too much interest though. I've pretty much stopped, it wasn't helping me understand them or what is going on at all," Ansel looks rather sheepishly up at Schwarz then ducks further into the Palace, escaping into his own embarrassment. Schwarz just watches him go, completely puzzled by his human. Maybe one day he'd understand them, but for now, he would just have to be puzzled.

Chapter 46

All too soon, the day of deployment is upon them. Schwarz wants to get out onto the field before the battle is to occur and see for himself that everything is as planned. All too many times he has gone onto a field expecting one thing, only to find another thing. While it has been well known for generations of fighters that no plan lasts initial actions, the landscape itself does not necessarily change, and he wants to be familiar with that before tackling his adversary, Pluie.

Schwarz has no doubt that Pluie had already seen the battlelines, and has studied all of the maps. He fully expects Pluie to have a play-by-play detailed battle plan with alternative actions for almost every contingency. He was always a heavy planner. It tends to work for him. Schwarz is just hoping his chaotic battle nature will be enough to throw a wrench in his plans, as the humans say.

It is Ansel who finds him first before he departs. Ansel, carrying a bookbag and a heavy coat. "Where do you think you're going?" Schwarz asks him as he finishes packing the last of his armor. The trucks that are going to haul his stuff for him are due to arrive soon. It is rather nice that he is not going to have to fly his own gear in for once. Modern life can be so much more convenient than the "olden" days.

"I'm coming with you," Ansel answers back. "You did not think you were going to have a dragon battle and exclude me, did you? I want to see it. Besides,

I've never seen another dragon before. I want to see what he looks like."

"I fully expected to leave without you. It will be far too dangerous to take you onto a battlefield. You have absolutely no experience. You don't even have instincts for this if what the soldiers say is correct. When you were almost kidnapped, you stood there, moving only because you were thrown into the car. No, you're not going." There, it is settled. Sure, he made it sound like Ansel and Hannah might be going a couple of weeks ago, but things have changed and they're definitely not going now.

"Sure, I'm going. If you don't take me, one of the many transport vehicles will find room for me, I'm sure. Or I'll drive myself. I know where you guys are going. I'm not missing this. Besides, you told Hannah and me that we could go when this whole thing started" Ansel sets his bag down next to Schwarz's.

Ansel's bag is considerably smaller but similar in design to Schwarz's. Both bags are of brown suede material, tough and durable, and not prone to getting dirty. Both bags are waterproof and have a flap to cover the opening. The difference is the closures. Ansel's zipped and there is not a zipper large enough in the world to close Schwarz's, so it has a drawstring. In addition, where Ansel's suede material is soft to the touch and pliable, Schwarz's is stiffened and has many small seams where the various pieces had been joined to create a single large piece.

A smaller, purple canvas bag soon joins them as Hannah joins in. "I'm going, too." Ansel wants to argue with Hannah and tell her that it is too dangerous. BUT, self-preservation and logic intervened. Telling Hannah that she could not do something was never a great idea, at least not by him. She would have no problem beating him into submission, either intellectually or physically. She might be tiny, but she is fierce. And if he told her that it is dangerous, Schwarz would simply tell him the same thing, leaving them both in the Palace.

"Things have changed. There is no room for you. I'm not taking the harness and you can't travel with me without one. Unless you want to ride in the bag?" Schwarz used this argument once. It was effective. He rather doubted it would be effective this time, but at least he would try.

Hannah and Ansel both just glared up at him. "I'll ride in the truck, thank you." Hannah eventually answers. She has read about a couple dragon battles in her book, Dragon's Ring by Dave Freer. She wants to see if they are anything like the book. Plus, she wants to see if the other dragon has the same body shape as Schwarz.

In most of the books she's read, dragons have all different shapes. She could not picture a species that looked vastly different from individual to individual. Even humans all have the same basic body structure, if numerous variations on that structure. Dogs, designed to look different for different tasks, were obviously dogs. Were dragons like tigers, all having the same features, but slight variations, or more like dogs, with vast differences, or more like people, same forms with less pronounced differences?

"If I tell you no, explain that you would be in danger, and possibly put more people in danger as they try to protect you, would you please stay here?" Schwarz takes a completely different tactic. He has never used this tactic before, but hey, it might work. Looking at Hannah's determined state, he is pretty sure it wouldn't work on her, and if she goes, Ansel would go. She would go if her brother went or not, he is sure of it.

"We'll stay out of the way. We will stand where you tell us to, and move only if we are approached by the enemy. But, this should be a safer battle. No one is supposed to use any live fire. No one is actually supposed to get hurt. It is all for show against Pluie. The biggest danger will be when you are fighting Pluie, but you said you were going to try to subdue him, rather than kill him," Ansel answers. He is willing to give concessions to make everyone feel more comfortable about him watching. Provided he is still able to see everything, live, not just on a screen. Not that he would not be hoping that people were recording.

"You know Pluie is as big as me. We will be FIGHTING. This means, that things will get damaged, there will be blood, hopefully not guts. The town could easily be destroyed simply by the two of us fighting, people could be hurt unintentionally. We're hoping to have everyone cleared from the area when Pluie takes the stage, but there is no guarantee, and we won't be able to stop and move ourselves or others if they are in the way.

"Even if you start in a safe location, you could quickly find yourself in the danger zone. You will have to be prepared to move, very quickly if that is the case. I would be very upset to find that you have been squished because you froze up and forgot to move. If kidnapping you would have caused an international incident, can you imagine what you being squished by a French dragon will do?" Schwarz wants them to understand the reality. Yes, the plan is for no humans to get hurt. Schwarz is actually anticipating casualties approaching the three-digit marker. He is hoping it does not hit the four-digit mark, but he would not have been surprised if it did. He just hopes none of the casualties are actually fatalities.

"We will be careful. We will stay in the vehicles, or bunkers, and be prepared to move if it looks like we are in any type of danger, from Pluie or anyone else. If you know we are going, you won't have to worry about us sneaking in. If you put us with the military, they can watch over us, and make sure we don't do anything stupid. I'm sure that a couple babysitters can be spared to watch over us," Hannah says, being as reasonable as she can possibly be. She knows that they are going to win this one, that Schwarz would have no choice but to let them come. Ansel is far less sure. He remembers being locked in his room that first night.

"Fine. BUT, you will remain at the end of the train. You will remain off the field, several miles away. You will not get to see the battle up close. You would most likely see more from here, using those screens, but if you want to come along, fine. I don't really want to lock you guys in your rooms. If I don't come home, you will die a very slow and unpleasant death. No one wants that." Schwarz turns away from them, finishing his packing, making sure that he has everything he might need. Better to bring it and not need it than not to bring it and wish he had it.

"What do you mean, if you don't come home?" Hannah has a pretty good idea of what that means, but that would be acknowledging something she did not want to think about.

"Well, while we are busy planning on how to prevent loss of life and how to create a fake battle, Pluie is thinking about creating the Holy Roman Empire again. Death is something he is willing to risk for any of his people. I'm going to fight him with the intention of subduing him, dominating him, and making him give up. He's going to be fighting to find out the color of my intestines. I'm hoping to make it out alive. It is my plan to make it out without serious injury. But, plans often go awry."

"There is a real chance you could die?" Ansel has not actually thought about that. He is surprised by how sad that made him feel.

"There is always a chance of death when you enter a battlefield," Schwarz sits down, looking at the siblings. He tries to temper his words by giving a soft little chuckle, but the truth is, he could die. While mundane things could not kill a dragon, or even injure one, another dragon is hardly mundane.

"What happens to us, if you die? I go back to my old life, or..." Ansel is working himself up to actual anxiety. A few months ago, he would have almost welcomed a dragon battle so that he could return home, but now, he is worried that he could not go home. He is also worried for his friend, Schwarz. Someone that until recently he had not even realized he had started to count as a friend, and not a jailer.

Schwarz looks at Ansel, watches his anxiety grow, and realizes that the man is scared, not only for himself but for Schwarz as well. Schwarz wants to pull him close and comfort him, but he needs to answer the questions. Instead, he drops his head so that he is level with Ansel and speaks in a low, comforting tone. "IF, and this is only an if, I die you are entitled to the Palace for the time of a year. No one can come and take things from this Palace without your permission any time before that. After the year is over, you are to leave for wherever you want to go.

"If I die, I suggest you invest the gold that I have in the treasury in one of your banks. Bauer can help smooth the way, I think. Then sell off anything you are not attached to, if you want. Buy a nice place, and live in comfort and happiness. That is the best I can offer you, and it is what I would want for you. If you want to go back to the farm, you can, and with the money you will have, you can make it a very nice, comfortable farm with all the wood you need without hauling it from the forest yourself." That last bit is a reference to how they met, and it makes both of them feel a sense of nostalgia.

"For my part, I am going to my level best to not die. I am also hoping that Papillon does not let it even get to the point where there is a serious chance of death. That dragon might not be interested in politics or territory, but there is not a sane creature alive or dead who is not afraid of her. And, she's my sister. I'm very much hoping that the blood is thicker than wine." His words do the trick, Ansel has a slight smile and he seems to have relaxed a bit.

"Yeah, sisters can be terrifying," Ansel agrees. He feels better knowing that there is a plan if everything should go wrong, but he is greatly hoping that nothing will go wrong.

47

Chapter 47

In a village known as Wismar, not the scenic town of Wismar, just a tiny town with the same name, dust and dirt rolled through the streets. It is quiet. Very quiet. There is no noise coming from the homes that dot the streets. No cars are driving up or down the roads. The normal noises of dogs and children are absent. This is a town that was barely alive before and completely dead now. Everyone who lived in that town had been evacuated, if they wanted to go or not.

The few living beings that are left in that town, a couple dogs and cats, and one rabbit, all found new homes. Those new homes are with the various German Army units that now sit a couple miles back from that town. The soldiers take an immediate liking to the few animals that they find. There is even a husky now running around in his own uniform, happily prancing around the men, reducing the stress of those surrounding him with every stride.

Those same soldiers all know that the battle is supposed to be fake, a mock invasion. They all know the dangers that blank cartridges pose though. They also know the chances of a live round getting mixed in as well. They also know that the town itself has been rigged with various explosives to make it look and feel more like a live battle, rather than like a play. It has to convince a dragon, after all.

Schwarz drops down just outside of the encampment just as Ansel and

Hannah's vehicle pulls in. He has purposefully hung back with the caravan, making sure that his people arrive safely and that they are installed in a safe location. He does not like them being this close to the battle, but he rather doubted that even the fiercest of their battles would range three miles. Schwarz would just have to make sure that if they did take to the air, it was away from this location.

He does have to admit, it was nice having others carry his war gear. Normally, he would have to fly with his armor on, which was taxing, and carry the rest in his bag. It reduces his maneuverability considerably and makes him a target. This is easier and safer. He also has to admit, that he was rather glad Ansel is here. Ansel could help him with his armor, and while he hates to admit it, he needs the emotional support of a friend, Ansel provides that as well. Schwarz wonders if Ansel realizes how much he has come to care for that little human.

It is late afternoon by the time everyone is settled. The battle is set for the morning, just before dawn. France's army would cross into the town, and then they would "retaliate." Schwarz would not enter the scene until Pluie did. Once Pluie enters the scene, everyone else is to leave, limiting casualties. This is one of the most planned and choreographed battles that Schwarz had ever heard of, let alone engaged in. That is the plan, and with God's Grace -not that Schwarz believed in a god-, it would work.

Ansel and Hannah are to stay in the mobile bunker that the generals are staying in during the battle. None of the generals are happy to see the pair. They had assumed that they were staying home, safe. They would have preferred that they stayed home. The general view is that the siblings are people who have to be babysat and kept comfortable when the generals were busy trying to make sure their people are safe. At least they have their own tent to sleep in, rather than demanding special accommodations from the already frazzled quartermasters.

With Ansel and Hannah being one less thing that Schwarz has to worry about, he lays down by the bunker to try to get some sleep before dawn. It is a definite trial, getting some rest. While the German Army is instructed to ignore the dragon as much as possible, everyone knows that the order is absolutely impossible to enforce. Even if you were to put guards and a quarantine area for Schwarz, there are going to be people who had to see him for themselves. Schwarz did his best to mitigate this by using his powers to deflect notice. There are still those who saw him, and they simply had to approach him.

"Holy shit, there really is a dragon here," one soldier comments to himself as he approaches Schwarz.

"Holy shit, there is a person," Schwarz answers back, deadpan. He cracks his eyes open, dramatically, just like he had seen Smaug do it in the Hobbit movie that Ansel showed him. The look of the startlement is worth it, every time. So often people assume that because you look like a beast, you have the abilities and intelligence of one as well. Did no one ever read the stories of dragons? They are filled with intelligent, speaking dragons.

"You talk!" the man squeaked back.

"You hear," Schwarz may have played this game too many times. He slid his eyes shut once again, dismissing the man.

"Uh, um... I'm sorry to bother you. I just had to see for myself this dragon that everyone was talking about. Most of the guys think that it is some type of new rocket system. It would almost make sense, but why would we use a rocket system in a training scenario. Then when I looked over, I seemed to be the only one in my group that could see you, an actual dragon."

"Now you see me. You will most likely see the other dragon that we are here to appease as well. Your friends may or may not see him, too. If I were you, I would continue believing in the rocket system, whatever that happens to be. It would be easier for you now and in the long run."

With Schwarz's final words, the man turns and leaves, satisfied to have seen a dragon, but let down by the pure dismissal the dragon gave him. This scene is repeated several times that night by several other men and women, all of whom are absolutely certain they are not seeing what they think they are seeing, and in fact, finding that they are seeing what they thought they saw. They might have had a better time of it if they had gone to Ansel first, but he was camped behind Schwarz, and not easy to see while in the tent, and when he is awake, he is confined to the bunker. It is just as Schwarz preferred it.

48

Chapter 48

It is the azure time of day, just before true dawn. A light blue tint permeates the air, making everything look ghostly and haunted. It suits the mood perfectly. The air itself is still, and the only noise for miles is the howling of the husky. Schwarz had gone hunting while the skies were still black. Ansel had awoken before Schwarz made it back, and has a coffee in hand, and a finished plate of breakfast set aside when Schwarz lands, full after a successful hunt.

"Pluie is getting ready as we speak. I could see his encampment, absolutely ablaze with light. Help me into my armor, and then take Hannah and stay safe in the bunker," Schwarz says as a greeting to Ansel. His manner is brisk. Gone was the light-hearted being that Ansel is so accustomed to dealing with.

"Uh, okay," Ansel is caught off guard. He did not think that they would be moving quite so fast. He expected a little bit of time between breakfast, and battle, but as he looks around he could see people getting themselves ready. Armor is being strapped on, rifles checked, and equipment distributed.

Schwarz had spent some time with Ansel and Hannah, going over how to best strap on the armor. Schwarz could, and has, put it on by himself, but it is much easier to have help. Halfway through Ansel putting the breastplate on Schwarz, Hannah wakes up and helps. She is obviously bleary before her coffee and breakfast, but she figures that coffee could wait until they are done.

Once all but the helm is on, Ansel stands back and looks at Schwarz in full.

He is wearing battle armor that had seen combat before. It is not elegant or flashy like his enameled armor. This is plain steel, brushed and oiled so that it did not reflect the light as much as polished steel would have. It covers Schwarz's chest and back with cutouts for his wings. Large-scale plates ride down Schwarz's spine, ending just after the base of his tail. Similar plates ride up the front and back of his neck. All of it is articulated to give Schwarz the best range of motion possible while protecting him as much as possible. Impressive is hardly a strong enough word for the impression of Schwarz in full armor.

Now all there is for Schwarz to do is wait. While he stands there, Ansel and Hannah are allowed to sit with him, but they know as soon as he leaves they are to go immediately to the bunker. As the azure time ends and the sun breaks through the skies on its ascent, Schwarz's attention leaves his humans and turns to the battlefront.

***

Ernst Schmeid just joined the Army the year before. He had plans. He wanted to make the Army his career. He wanted to lead people, help people, save people. He was young, full of hope and ideals. He was naive. This is not even a real battle, this is a play, and he hates it. The blanks that they are firing at the "enemy" are loud. They echo through the deserted streets causing him to become disoriented. His group is running from place to place, fast. "Shrapnel" is flying from various walls and floors as the pre-positioned small explosives go off.

Schmeid might have once wanted to be in the Army. He might have wanted to be a soldier. He did well enough in boot camp. He did well enough in all the extra training he had. Nothing prepared him for this. And it is not even the real deal. *There was no way I could ever handle the real thing*, he thought to himself. Everyone else looked calm, cool, collected. Yeah, they look like they had an adrenaline dump like him, but they are definitely handling it better, he thinks.

Then his squad leader, Muller, drops. The laser tag system that they were using to determine if they were hit or not, beeped. A red light is shown from his harness. Muller is dead. If it had been yellow for critical, or blue for slightly, Schmeid could have handled it. Nope. He was dead. Schmeid is in charge. He looks around in panic, this could not be happening to him. Yeah, he thought he was prepared to command, if necessary.

Turning and looking at his fellow squadmates, he makes a split-second decision. "Grab him, no man left behind. We have to finish the mission. We just have to get to that building over there and defend it. Once we're there, we'll radio in and see what they want done." *That's what Muller would have done, right?* He hopes he is making the right decision. He is definitely requesting a change in orders as soon as this is done. He is so not cut out for this.

Every crisis is like this. A problem, a moment to react, and a decision to make. Muller is the last "casualty" that the squad suffers. The echoes from the various blanks and explosions eventually began to die down. They have survived their mock encounters. It is time to head back. Muller would have to be carried out, but as soon as they got picked up by the trucks, the exercise would be over. It really is not that bad. Nothing he would ever be comfortable in, but Schmeid feels more confident than he had ever felt before. This was something he could do.

As the sun hits its highest point, a great roar echoes down the streets of Wismar. It stops nearly everyone in their tracks. Even the newly confident Schmeid and his squad stop. This roar is accompanied by a following one, just as loud as the first. It almost reminds Schmeid of the roaring that the lions would do at the zoo, long, coughing-like roars. As the sound continues, it reminded him more and more of that zoo lion. He knows what it is though, it is the dragon that they had been warned about.

Everyone begins to run then. The exercise is over. Muller is up and following Schmeid as he leads the way to the trucks. He could see other units heading that way as well. They have a vehicle that they were designated to ride in, he does not see it though. Coming to a stop, he looks around. He thought he was scared before. He had not even seen the dragon, but the sound of it was enough to send him running.

There, there is the truck, they have to move. Within moments they are in the truck and riding away from the city, towards the encampment three miles away. They would be safe in a matter of minutes, but it still feels too long. It feels even longer as he watches the giant shadow of another dragon pass over them. Schwarz is taking the field.

49

Chapter 49

The moment that Schwarz has been waiting for finally has come. Pluie has walked into the city. He has taken the stage. With a wave of his head, he warns Ansel and Hannah to go back towards the bunker. He donned his mighty horned helm and takes to the air in a single bound. He is off to do battle. It is exhilarating. It is terrifying. It is necessary.

Schwarz goes high, much higher than he normally flies with Ansel. He wants to be out of sight of Pluie. He can hear Pluie's coughing roars. He is claiming the town as his. He likely assumes that Schwarz would not do battle over such a small place, but he is wrong. Once Schwarz is over top of the shining blue dragon in his brilliant blue enameled armor, he strikes.

Schwarz comes down fast and hard, striking Pluie from above and behind, knocking the other dragon down, and driving him down the street. Buildings crumble, roads are dug up, and there will be no recovery for Wismar. The shockwave of the strike is felt in the German camp. It is not enough to incapacitate the French dragon though as Schwarz had hoped. It is enough to enrage him though. Schwarz had air breaked right before impact, not wanting to kill Pluie, but rather hoping to knock him down enough that he would submit and back off.

"Coward! You struck from behind! And look what you did to my armor!" Pluie roars. He gestures towards his elaborate chest plate. The scratches are horribly obvious against the highly polished surface. Schwarz could not bring himself to care though. This is a dragon who is making life miserable for everyone, and who fancies himself an emperor.

"Oh, so sorry! Did you get a boo-boo?" Schwarz mocks before rushing forward and continuing his attack. Pluie is either not fast enough to dodge, or he chooses not to dodge. The result is the same either way, the two crash, chest to chest. Their hind talons dig into the ground, leaving deep gouges. Their wings beat, and their teeth snap, grappling with the plates on their neck and shoulders. They suddenly tore apart, facing opposite directions than they had initially started facing, breathing hard and fast. In battle, a few minutes feels like hours, and for beings the size of dragons, it feels like days.

Rearing back, high on his hind legs, Pluie lets his wings flair. He is an impressive sight, terrible to behold. What is even worse was the sudden darkening of the skies. What was a clear, bright day suddenly becomes overcast. The rain, thunder, and lightning that struck mere seconds after he rose is terrifying to everyone but Schwarz. As the thunder rose, he strikes once again, this time diving low.

Schwarz dove under Pluie, twisting in mid-lunge and folding his wings under him. He rakes up and under Pluie's armor, scoring heavy, but not life-threatening injuries. He is doubly eager to get the battle done. Fighting is hard work, fighting in the rain while dodging lightning is nearly impossible. He is prepared when Pluie drops down onto him, kicking hard with his hind legs while levering himself up and turning his opponent.

A hard kick from Pluie sends Schwarz skidding away from him. It frees some room for Pluie to attack, but also gives Schwarz enough room to deploy his own special skill, Darkness. Reaching out with his right while pulling his left claw in towards his chest, he takes the sight away from Pluie who comes to a sudden stop. "Do you think that this will save you, whelp? I will defeat you no matter what. You have been a thorn in my side for an eon, sight is not necessary to kill you. I can smell you!" he screams as he shifts his head back and forth, hunting by sound and smell for his adversary.

Schwarz for his part holds very still, hoping that Pluie would lose him in the noise of the rain while he tries to catch his breath. It has been forever since he had fought, and he is not the young dragonling that he was at the time. If he does not end this soon, both of them will die. For his part, Pluie is intent on just Schwarz dying that day as he calls lightning and rain in absolute abundance. If he could not see, neither shall Schwarz.

The curtain of lightning that Pluie calls upon comes bearing down on both of the dragons. Schwarz looks around, trying to find an escape as he watches what could be his death rolling towards him. He rushes forward, unable to find escape, and strikes Pluie in the joint between his helm and neck plates with all of the force that his sword-length teeth could deliver. The lightning stops as both dragons crash to the ground under the powerful talons of Papillon.

50

Chapter 50

T he whole world freezes. No one, not human nor dragon, had expected Papillon to take the stage. She is known to be a pacifist. She is peaceful, always trying to get people not to fight, and not to hurt others. She is also the sister to Schwarz and the mate to Pluie. She has too much to lose by letting them kill each other. She decides to put an end to it.

Holding both dragons down she raises her own powerful golden wings, dispelling both the storm that Pluie called, and the darkness that Schwarz had cast. The sky takes on the color of saffron, almost a reflection of her orange scales. She snarls down at the two dragons that she holds with apparent ease and they both immediately submit to her, absolutely refusing to fight the dragon who held them down. Neither of them are that stupid or bloodthirsty.

"I was willing to go along with this whole scheme thinking you two could fight it out like adults. I figured that you two would clash, fight for a minute, and then you would realize that there was nothing to gain by killing each other.

"Pluie, you told me you would not try to kill my brother. Schwarz, I expected better." No human could understand her. She spoke not French nor German, but rather the first language of the world, Dragon.

"I was apparently wrong. It may have started out as a dominance fight between you two hot heads, but that curtain of lightning and that last strike to the throat were both killing blows. Did you honestly think that I was going to let you two fight to the death? You made me get involved with this whole thing. I was enjoying my chocolate!" Papillon puts a little extra downward force onto the two dragons as she finishes that last statement. She, like her humans, enjoys her chocolate.

"Now, Pluie and Schwarz. I'm going to let you two up. You will apologize for allowing your behavior to get so out of hand. You will apologize to the humans for ruining their perfectly good village. You will go home. We are not campaigning through Europe. We are not redoing the Holy Fucking Roman Fucking Empire. I'm over it. Got it?" That last question was not really a question, but the two males tried to nod their heads anyway.

With that, both Schwarz and Pluie pull themselves from the ground, rubbing at the various scrapes that Papillon administered to them. Neither one of them looked at each other or at Papillon. "Say you're sorry for attacking Germany," she admonishes Pluie. He for his part grumbles an apology. "Try again." She is insistent. She is over this and is tired of dealing with adults who want to act like adolescents.

"I'm sorry for attacking Germany. Sorry for trying to restart the Holy Roman Empire," Pluie finally apologizes in a clear voice, even if he does not look at Schwarz as he did. Instead, he keeps his eyes down, focused on the boulder that he is rolling around in front of him. He glances up at Papillon though as he speaks. He needs to know if she considers that a proper apology, or if he is going to have to go further. He had also uses Dragon to apologize. If Papillon is going to use it, then it was only right that all of them use it.

"Schwarz?" her voice is crystal clear and not quite demanding. It was hardly a questioning tone though.

"I accept your apology. Sorry for staging a fake battle for you. Sorry for letting the fight get out of hand and for scratching your armor," Schwarz does look at Pluie as he speaks. His Dragon speech was clear and concise. He keeps his bearing straight and proud. He is not going to slump and relax just yet. He wants to look like he could have won that fight, although he is not actually so sure that he could have. Either way, he is not going to be completely cowed by his sister, no matter how fearsome she might be.

186

"Good. Pluie, please head back to La Flotte. I will join you shortly. I need to handle some things here, and I would like to talk to my brother." Papillon backs up, giving Pluie enough room to launch into the sky. He does not do that though, instead, he rounds on Schwarz with words rather than talons.

"Staging a fake battle?! What are you talking about?"

"Whoops," Schwarz quietly says to himself. Speaking to Pluie he answered, "You did not actually think that the people of Germany and France would actually fight, did you? From what I gather, they are allies. There would be repercussions if they were to fight. No, all of this was a play for you. A way to prevent unnecessary death and destruction, while still fulfilling your demands."

"Schwarz, you never could keep your mouth shut," Papillon mutters as Pluie begins to stomp and rage.

"You mean to tell me that my own people went behind my back and arranged a fake battle with your people? That all of this was planned? Do they think that they can so disrespect me?!" Pluie screams. His language slipped back and forth between French and Dragon, displaying his irritation. For his part, Schwarz actually does keep his mouth shut and does not answer him.

"That's it! When I get back to Paris, I'm flooding it! They made me look like a fool! How dare they think that they can disrespect the Emperor of France like this! Do they not know that they lead at my sufferance!" Pluie had lapsed completely into French by the time he was done ranting and threatening France. Schwarz watches him with dawning horror on his face, while Papillon watches him pace back and forth in his rage completely dispassionately. She might kill him herself.

"Are you done?" She intones in Dragon. Ice might have shattered with how cold her voice is. At the sound of his impending death, Pluie stops and looks at Papillon, really looking at her. She is not amused. She is not even angry. She is deadly cold and he could feel the ice under him crack. He'd better watch his step. There are few things as terrifying in this world or the next as a woman, human or dragon, that is done with your shit.

Pluie seems to shrink into himself. He glances over to Schwarz as though seeking some type of help against Papillon, but Schwarz is a smart dragon and stays out of it, mouth shut. "Yes, Pappi, I'm done," Pluie answers in the smallest voice he could. He might be an idiot some of the time, but no one is stupid enough to be an idiot all of the time, especially with Papillon.

"What are you going to do?" Papillon's voice took on the same tone that a child might hear from their kindergarten teacher. It hits Pluie the same way that it hits the children. He knows that he is in the wrong and the only way out is to do what she tells him to do.

"I'm going to La Flotte and waiting for you."

"Exactly. Now off with you."

Pluie does not hesitate this time. He walks a little ways off of the pair, looks back once, sighs, and throws himself into the air. It is only when he passes his own encampment that he thinks to apply his magic and render himself unseen. Not that it matters, the videos of the two dragons fighting are already making themselves known throughout the world. This time there is physical evidence.

51

Chapter 51

Papillon does not stay back to lecture Schwarz. Instead, she holds back so that she an talk to her brother, whom she has missed for so long. "I really wished that we could have gone to visit you while you were cursed. Unfortunately, if I had even entered into the woods, I would have been as cursed as you. Every message I sent to you was returned with the blood of my messenger. I could not risk it."

"I understand, sister. The magic that bound me was very extensive. Not to mention the threats that came from Easifat Ramlia and his first in command, Rasul. I was fortunate that there was a human who went out in the dark, looking for wood, and managed to get lost," Schwarz looks over at his sister fondly. She is one of two that he had left from his clutch. Their parents both had moved onto the next plane shortly after raising them to independence, so Papillon and Tàiyáng Yuèguò are it. Maybe one day he would go visit old Yang, but not now.

"Is your savior here? I can not imagine you not keeping him close. I had heard it was a boy."

"Ansel? You want to meet Ansel?" Schwarz signals over to the nearest vehicle, calling them over. "Please bring Ansel, and Hannah while you're at it. Papillon would like to meet them."

It is mere minutes before Ansel and Hannah appear in a cloud of dust and dirt with Ansel in the driver's seat. Schwarz is absolutely certain that he stole the vehicle from whatever military person was supposed to fetch him. He could not imagine anyone letting such a valuable asset drive himself up to a potential threat, even with Schwarz to protect him. But, no matter what happened, the siblings arrive.

"Ansel, Hannah, I would like to present you to my sister, Papillon. She is the Butterfly of the Dragons, queen in her own right, Lady of France. I am absolutely certain I am forgetting about a hundred more titles, but the most important ones are Friend and Sister. Papillon, please allow me to present Ansel and Hannah. They are brother and sister, although he is the only one that is rightfully mine."

"It is a great pleasure to meet you two. Thank you, Ansel, for freeing my brother of his curse, even if it resulted in you being cursed with him for the rest of your life. At least it will be an interesting life, as it were. I am forever at your disposal if you should need me. Simply call my name, with intent, upon the winds, and my namesakes shall see that I hear you." Papillon then surprises Ansel by bowing to him, tucking her right arm under herself, much like he has seen horses bow. It made him feel quite uncomfortable to receive such honor from such a magnificent dragon.

"Being tied to Schwarz isn't so bad. I have already experienced so much more than I ever would have otherwise. It sure beats cutting wood at the farm." Ansel tries to make light and deflect his unease, but as he speaks, he notices Hannah looking at the ground where the two dragons fought. In particular where Papillon held Schwarz and Pluie down.

"Where did the gold come from?" Hannah asks. Ansel walks over to where she stands, and there it is, two puddles of gold.

"Well, on the very rare times that we bleed, our blood turns to gold once it touches the air. I am absolutely certain that I will be raining gold as I fly back to the Palace in the Mount. I am also certain that we will clean the battlefield and remove any traces of gold that we might find. We don't want people thinking to harm us to get to our blood. Although we cannot be hurt by mundane means, I don't want someone deciding that they would like to test that theory with modern heavy weapons. It might hurt.

"Nor do I want them to go after smaller Magickals, ones whose blood does not turn to gold, and harm them trying to get rich. I would appreciate it if you told no one about what you learned. There are too many creatures who might be hurt if this were to get out." As Schwarz speaks, he plucks the two puddles of gold out of the ground and deposits them in a bag at his waist. What gold does not fit in his bag, he places in Papillon's care.

"I wouldn't tell. There is no good to be had by telling such an incredible thing. Besides, it is not like anyone would believe me. That's not even part of the normal mythology for dragons," Hannah answers as she hands him a small nugget that she found. Schwarz smiles at her and presses it back into her hands.

"You can keep that one. Consider it a keepsake."

"We should offer to give the gold to the people of Wismar. They lost their town in this mock battle," Ansel suggests. "It's not like we don't have enough gold at home."

"That is so sweet of you, Ansel," Papillon answers. "However, the repairs will come out of Pluie's stash. As will any fees or fines that might come from the Unseen Treaty, although I am pretty sure that the treaty is pretty well null and void now. There has been too much exposure to ever attempt to go into hiding again."

"Thank you, sister. We had better be going back. I'm exhausted. Pluie put up a hell of a fight and I'm not young anymore. Feel free to visit the Mount sometime. My door is always open to you," Schwarz says. With that, he gathers his people and departs the battlefield for home.

52

EPILOGUE

I t is finally quiet at The Palace in the Mount. Schwarz is recovering from his injuries that he sustained while battling with Pluie. Ansel is able to relax without the stress of state officials coming to their home every time he turned around. Elisabeth Bauer retired as Chancellor and was replaced by Olaf Scholz. Camille Dupont picked up Matteo Moulin. All the loose stings that had needed to be tied had been tied. There is peace.

***

Half a world away, the same could not be said in Saudi Arabia. Those sands tremble with a rage that had not been seen in hundreds of years, if not longer. Rasul finds himself prostrate in the marble chamber that Easifat Ramlia called home. All of Easifat's plans had been drained away like sand in an hourglass, and someone is going to have to pay for it. Rasul only hopes it is not him.

Ahead of him, Easifat Ramlia paces. Every footfall can be felt through the stone floor. Every turn of the great dragon blew a gail's worth of wind across the wide room. Tapestries that had once hung with pride now litter the floors, tossed aside in the dragon's rage. Fires that have burned for generations have gone out, snuffed by his fury.

"The Unseen Treaty is destroyed. That stupid stunt that Pluie and Schwarz did in Wismar showed the world, beyond a doubt, that we exist. It will only be a matter of time before the masses begin to suspect that other Magickals exist. Everything I have built, every peace brokered, gone, shattered!" Rasul could feel the marble shatter under Easifat's front legs at this proclamation, emphasizing his point. There will be hell to pay.

***

Back at Hannah's farm, another discussion is taking place. This one is full of the same drama but lacks an element of violence. This one is between Otto and Hannah's mother and just might change the path of Hannah and Ansel's lives.

"The time for hiding is done. Your mission is complete. You did not fail. No one expected the curse to be held for two hundred years. It is time for you to come home. It is time for your children to learn who they are," Otto tries to convince the woman in front of him.

Gone is her glamor, hiding her pointed ears and youthful appearance. Here, in the privacy of her kitchen, in the early hours before Hannah arrives home, Corrinne looks exactly like what she is, an elven warrior. Her glossy blond hair, normally swept up into a tight bun at the top of her head, hangs loose. Her arms, normally covered in loose-fitting fabrics are bare, allowing the world to see solid muscle, honed by centuries of sword work.

"I am their mother. I will decide if they are ready to learn that they are not strictly human. In the elven world, they would be barely seen as more than toddlers. It will be a sudden shift for a pair of young adults who have already experienced so much change recently." Corrinne counters.

"The time of hiding is done either way. The Unseen Treaty has been demolished. Schwarz and Pluie could not have destroyed it more completely if they had set out to do so. Now, now we must do what we can to control and contain the backlash. Hiding the truth from them will only put them in more danger. I cannot allow Hannah to be in danger." Otto slaps the table to emphasize his words. Neither of them heard the car pull into the driveway or Hannah open the door.

"What danger?" she asks in a quiet voice. She didn't hear everything, but she heard enough. "And who are you, and where is Mom?"

www.ingramcontent.com/pod-product-compliance
Lightning Source LLC
Chambersburg PA
CBHW050532260626
47157CB00004B/1569